# A House Shaken

A Novel by Sam Markley

.

Note for Librarians: A cataloguing record for this book is available from Library
and Archives Canada at www.collectionscanada.ca/amicus/index-e.html

Printed in Victoria, BC, Canada.

ISBN: 9781-4269-129-1-7 (soft)
ISBN: 9781-4269-129-2-4 (hard)
ISBN: 9781-4269-129-3-1 (eBook)

*We at Trafford believe that it is the responsibility of us all, as both individuals
and corporations, to make choices that are environmentally and socially sound.
You, in turn, are supporting this responsible conduct each time you purchase a
Trafford book, or make use of our publishing services. To find out how you are
helping, please visit www.trafford.com/responsiblepublishing.html*

*Our mission is to efficiently provide the world's finest, most comprehensive
book publishing service, enabling every author to experience success.
To find out how to publish your book, your way, and have it available
worldwide, visit us online at www.trafford.com*

*Trafford rev: 7/2/2009*

 **www.trafford.com**

**North America & international**
toll-free: 1 888 232 4444 (USA & Canada)
phone: 250 383 6864 ♦ fax: 250 383 6804 ♦ email: info@trafford.com

# Chapter One

## THE HOUSE ON BROAD STREET

A SLAMMING DOOR can shake a whole house. That was the thought that ran through my mind as my sister, Pat, stormed up the stairs, stomped to her room and, as hard as she could muster, slammed her bedroom door. Wham!!

Within moments there was a response. Our father jumped from his easy chair where he had found refuge from a hectic day and ran to the foot of the stairs bellowing in his deepest, most sinister voice, "Young lady, you get down here. NOW!"

Pat was the rebel in the family and was close to becoming a teenage problem child. She was feisty and argumentative and not afraid to express her dissension with one of Dad's myriad rules. This explosion was about her curfew, insisting that she was living under a totally different set of rules from me, her little brother. My father was strict with his rules but inconsistent. The problem, as Pat saw it, was the inflexible, rigid set of rules for his three daughters and the more lenient, looser rules for his two sons.

Our quiet, peaceful street was located just minutes from the downtown area of Danville, but nonetheless provided a refuge from the busier commercial section. The white Colonial style of our home was typical of the area and represented the affluent part of town. The house was centrally located on the biggest lot on the street with woods bordering the property in the back. Our large yard was the gathering spot for the neighborhood kids, a place where all our games and activities began. Whether it was a conventional game of football, 'hide and seek', 'kick the can', 'hit the bat', or 'olly, olly, oxen free', our yard was always full of kids at play. Pat and her friends were constantly playing hopscotch on the sidewalk in front of the house or jumping rope, while the boys were doing their own thing or harassing the girls. As the neighborhood grew older, the games ceased and more relevant topics, such as curfews, became issues. Pat's friends had more liberal curfews and generally lived without many of the stringent rules that our father had put in place. It was just a matter of time before Pat was going to rebel. Tonight's explosion was not unexpected.

The house indeed shook from the slamming door. It sounded like a gun had gone off. The ensuing yelling added to the drama and further disrupted the tranquility of a quiet evening. I wondered how much of this chaos was noticed by our neighbors. I imagined them referring to those Cassidy kids as "a wild bunch."

Inside the house, there were different concerns. Confrontations with a disgruntled daughter were not only an event that was closely monitored by the other four children, but also served as a launching pad for one of my father's impassioned speeches on the rights of his children to defy his commands. We braced for the inevitable argument. Pat's insistence that she lived under a totally different set of rules from her brothers was quickly dismissed by our father, igniting her explosion. Dad was 100 per cent Irish with a quick temper and little tolerance for insubordination. He never lost these occasional challenges to his authority for to do so would have undermined the very fabric of the discipline he was attempting to instill. Pat put on a good show, with some yelling and screaming, and a little crying; but in the end, my father prevailed. Trying to remain inconspicuous through all the commotion, I had cowered in the corner of the living room, hoping not to be noticed. Unfortunately, my father turned to me and asked my opinion, expecting me to agree with his position. However, I was quick to come to Pat's defense, something I got used to doing the rest of our lives. All it got me this time was a similar curfew and a two-week grounding. Our house was definitely not a democracy. I guess somehow the squeaky wheel got the grease and I got the shaft.

The Cassidy's were a well known family in town. Dad was the local Chevrolet dealer and a respected business man. At home, he was the absolute ruler. Mom was the sometimes less than enthusiastic supporter who invariably was cast in the role of reconciler. It was mom who held the family together with her sympathetic ear, her unconditional interest in everything each of her five children were doing, and her insistence that the entire family be present and on time for the evening meal.

My oldest sister, June, was Daddy's little girl who could do no wrong. Because of June's magnetic personality and her striking good looks, she was the most popular girl in her senior class at Danville High. She was chosen as the queen of senior prom and was an active member of the cheerleaders. She hosted numerous parties in our cellar where all the football players and cheerleaders danced the jitterbug to popular fifty's music played on her victrola. When she turned sixteen, my father bought her a brand new 1955 Bel Air convertible. It was an extraordinary sight to see June driving around town in her new car. She made quite an impression with her strikingly beautiful face and flaming red hair. Pat and I decided that June was going to be a tough act to follow, but we loved her to death because she always made time for us, even when she was surrounded by her friends. Yes, June was one of a kind.

In contrast, Chip, who was born a year after June, had a more difficult time. His nickname was given to him at birth because my father believed in that 'chip off the old block' nonsense. Chip never lived up to my father's lofty expectations of his first-born boy, and consequently, was the frequent target of much of my father's criticism. Whether it was justified or not, it was difficult to be in the same room with the two of them when my father began his diatribes on his perceived notion that Chip was a slacker.

Jaime was next, the third baby in three years. What Chip lacked in self-motivation, Jaime made up for with an incomprehensible desire to be the best at everything she did. She followed June's steps quite nicely in the popularity department, but added to that an insatiable quest for learning that bordered on obsessive. She was the top student in her class, a feat accomplished with a schedule of studying that began the minute our supper ended and lasted until my mother would tell her to turn out the lights and go to sleep. She was very quiet around the house, but like June, she also displayed a strong sense of the family unit and was always available and helpful to Pat and me. She set an academic standard in the family that was going to be impossible for her young siblings to match. In her four years of high school and her four years of college, she never received less than an "A". Pat and I came up short on that achievement our first marking period freshman year.

After June, Chip, and Jaime were born most families would have been complete, but it was the 1940's and the times dictated a change in the status quo. World War II ended in 1945. Its celebratory ending triggered a phenomenon known as the post war baby boom that would have a profound impact on the remainder of the Twentieth Century and beyond. Returning war heroes and their waiting brides copulated like rabid dogs in heat resulting in the most dramatic population explosion in history. Not a war veteran, but nonetheless a keen participant in the celebrations ending the war, my father restarted his family—with a little help from my mother. Pat was born in June of 1945, probably the result of anticipating a victory in Europe party. My mother was half German so I can imagine the drama that led up to Pat's conception. Mom always swore that she was German nobility somehow related to Kaiser Wilhelm, the head of Germany during World War I. Her credibility became questionable when she added that her family had once owned the island of Manhattan but were swindled out of it by unscrupulous land grabbers. There was only so much even a child could believe from their parents' stories, and she didn't help her cause with the uncontrollable smirk that accompanied all her tall tales. Unlike June and Jaime who were redheads, Pat was a brunette. Her different coloring was indicative of her different personality. She possessed a presence unbounded by convention. My father said she walked to the beat of a different drummer; but, to me, she was the leader of the band. We were kindred spirits and our souls are forever linked together.

I was the last child to come along, in November of 1946. Comparisons to Chip began almost immediately. He was eight years old when I was born but had done very little in that time to encourage my father's affection. He was not a good student; he was sloppy; and he did nothing to help around the house. He never did anything to stand out in a family of achievers. His first eight years had been wasted in establishing any kind of father-son relationship. As a result, Chip harbored resentment toward me from the beginning. It was a resentment that was fostered by the indelicate way my father treated him and the more favorable way he treated me. I had nothing to do with any of that, but it was obvious that my father perceived me to be more like June.

In a four-bedroom house with five kids and two parents there was some necessary room sharing. Chip and I shared a room in what was always an unholy alliance. Chip dealt with his ever growing hostility toward me by promising to "whip my ass" at the slightest provocation. It wasn't until I was in my early teens and playing on the high school football team that he realized that his threats were shallow boasts and his physical superiority was a figment of his imagination. Fortunately, nothing ever happened between us that provided what would have been an embarrassing episode for my older brother. Our contentious relationship actually improved over the years and as we got older, I honestly believe Chip took great satisfaction in some of my achievements, even though he would occasionally bring up some old bravado with a reflective: "you know I could still whip your ass".

Jaime and Pat also shared a room. They were two totally different personalities with diverse interests and motivations. Jaime was the serious intellect with the serious goals. Pat was the rebel, who studied only when she had to. She loved Elvis Presley and James Dean, and she would occasionally sneak out to join her friends in some good-natured partying. Regardless of their differences, Jaime and Pat shared a great sense of humor and formed a life-long bond cemented by Jaime's reluctance to squeal on Pat's after hours trips out the second story bedroom window and down the lattice work attached to the upstairs porch. It was Pat's resentment of my father's strict rules that led to her rebellious behavior, her temper tantrums and her infamous door slamming. As it turned out, my father had his reasons.

June, of course, had her own room and pretty much the run of the house. She was smart; she was pretty; she was dating the quarterback on the football team; and she was preparing to go on to college. And then came that memorable night when the rest of us awoke to her crying. My mother and father told us to all go back to bed. They said they were taking June to the hospital. None of us could sleep as we wondered what was wrong with June. The next day we had our answer as my mother told us June had delivered a premature baby boy. We were all in shock. I wondered how this was going to change our idyllic lives. I wondered how our sense of family and security in our house was going to be affected. One look at my father gave me my answer. He was crushed!

# Chapter Two

## BEANTOWN OR BUST

YOU READY FOR this?" Baxter said to me as we approached the outskirts of Boston. "The big city...where dreams are made."

"Or lost," I responded.

Baxter and I were high school buddies who pursued totally different career paths after graduation but always kept in close touch. We had planned for years to make our big breakout to city life and now, without the blessing of our families, Baxter and I were finally taking a shot at Beantown. As we drove in on the Southeast Expressway, the majestic sky scrapers loomed on the horizon promising us adventure and a pursuit of the unknown. We were like giddy little kids approaching a new playground.

"Do you realize how many girls live in Boston?" Baxter exclaimed seemingly pondering how he was going to meet them all.

While my buddy openly mused over the endless possibilities that awaited him, I worried that our planning which was woefully inadequate and our resources, which were even worse, would lead to our crawling back to Danville with our tails between our legs. We were winging this invasion and failure was more than a frightening possibility.

Baxter was a unique individual. He was an accomplished high school basketball player in spite of his 5ft. 4in. height. He dabbled at playing other sports, and otherwise was happily leading an undistinguished life that centered on an eternal desire to be tanned. His resume was empty but, in a sense, was also full because he was quite simply the best con artist I had ever seen. It's a rare individual who can say just about anything, however inappropriate, to any girl and not be the recipient of a good slap. His charming way and dark good looks were magnets to women. He was ready to try his hand at the girls of the city and his scrapbook was filled with small town success. I wondered if I would be able to keep up.

My experience with women was far less exciting compared to Baxter's. I planned on marrying my college sweetheart, cheated on her my second semester senior year on a dare, and was subsequently dumped on the eve of my graduation. With the help of a lot of alcohol, it only took me about ten years to get over it. At any rate, it was a convenient excuse for some erratic behavior after graduation, which put a whole bunch of stress on the relationship I had with my parents. When I announced to my mother and father my intentions to move to Boston, I almost felt their relief that I would, at least temporarily, be out of their hair. My mother put on a good front in trying to talk me out of the move but finally acquiesced with the parting advice to "do some growing up in Boston." My father, like Polonius to Laertes in Shakespeare's Hamlet, provided more meaningful advice. "Don't trust anyone; don't owe anybody anything; and don't lend anybody money." It was so typical of my father that his advice would end with the mention of money, for to him, money was as important as his children.

We exited into Boston and headed for the 4th floor apartment we had rented in the Fenway section, on Westland Avenue. Baxter and I were big Red Sox fans so the thought of living so close to Fenway Park was certainly a bonus even though we shared a great amount of space in our apartment with a rather healthy cockroach population. Our first week in the city was spent looking for jobs and acclimating ourselves to our new lives. I wasn't totally naïve at this time, but to say I was street-wise would have been a stretch. We lived off of Mass Avenue near the junction with Boylston

Street. The Prudential building, the highest in Boston at the time, hovered down the block. Restaurants, bars and coffee shops lined the street. There were people everywhere, scurrying about at a fast pace. We noticed that most of the people on the streets were young people with a direction and purpose to their step. In contrast, we were just a couple of country bumpkins searching for an identity in this unfamiliar concrete world. One thing that stood out above all else—there were lots of good-looking girls. Girls in mini-skirts, girls in hot pants, girls in thigh high boots--everywhere there were girls. All I could think of was that we weren't ready for all this. It was like trying to get to heaven with only a step ladder. Here we were in the midst of all these beautiful people with no jobs and very little money. We looked like tourists and acted like miscreants. We had to get jobs and get them quickly. But most of all, we had to start dressing and acting like we belonged.

It was 1969. The war in Vietnam was raging on. The evening news was filled with pictures of a war mission gone badly. Young soldiers were sent home in body bags to a troubled country filled with dissidents that had seemingly turned their backs on their fighting men. Public burning of draft cards and the American flag were a nightly occurrence on the news. Protests involving anti-war and anti-draft themes drew thousands of students from all corners of the city. Social change was in the air. Hair became a symbol of the student revolution with kids growing their hair to medieval lengths. The student protesters established their own fashion rebellion with psychedelic clothing that reflected a new culture—tie-dye shirts, bellbottom pants and the total disregard for the bra.

For Baxter and me, the draft day call had led us to join the Army National Guard back in Connecticut. Each month we would have to return to Connecticut for a weekend drill and two weeks in the summer we went to Camp Drum in New York for further combat training. One of the requirements of the Guard was that we keep our hair trimmed neatly and totally off the ears. Not only did we now live in a neighborhood in Boston that was surrounded by colleges and consequently, college students, but our National Guard haircuts made us stand out as "right wing conservative freaks!" We might have picked the wrong neighborhood in which to live.

The search for jobs was tedious. I was an English major in college; consequently I was looking for a job that bore some sort of semblance to what I had studied. I came close to landing an interesting position on a number of occasions only to lose out to someone from one of the forty colleges that existed within the confines of Boston. Desperate for any kind of meaningful work, I accepted a job in the Xerox copy center at the NASA building in Cambridge, just over the Charles River from Boston. The room I worked out of was in the bowels of the NASA building. It had three of the largest copying machines in existence. It was my job to make copies for the other sixteen floors in the building, collate them into nice little piles of scientific data and staple them for delivery to the appropriate office. A monkey could do it—but I believed, probably not as well. The job kept me in rent money with a little left over for groceries and entertainment. It also afforded me the opportunity to answer all inquiries from curious relatives and nosey friends as to where I worked with; "I work at NASA."

Baxter had far less trouble landing a job. He was a graduate of bartender's school and he was hired at the first bar that he applied. It was a typical neighborhood bar located across from the Prudential Building. His clientele were regulars and he used his boyish charm to gain their confidence. I too became a regular and watched with amazement how easily he handled these people and how quickly they took to him. He was definitely adapting to the city quicker than I was. It also seemed he was making much more money—so much for higher education. Our lives were changing quickly as we were beginning to settle into city life. We both had jobs, and we were making new friends. With the exception of our short hair, we believed we were fitting in.

# Chapter Three

## THE BROAD STREET FOLLIES

THE HOUSE ON Broad Street was a symbol of my father's success. He had purchased the Chevrolet dealership in town in the early 1940's when his partner died. Dad was a product of the Great Depression. A graduate of Boston University in 1933, he learned hard lessons of business during the worst of times. It is said of those that went through the Depression that the survivors could squeeze the buffalo off a nickel. He was notoriously frugal even during the economic boom of the 50's and 60's. There were no allowances to his kids even though we were expected to perform our chores in a timely and conscientious manner. One of his favorite platitudes, of which there were many, was "any job worth doing is worth doing well." As his troops in the household, we were expected to do our jobs without grumbling and, of course, without compensation. In the neighbors view, we were spoiled rich kids; but in reality, we were rich in family interaction and the physical trappings of a nice house in a nice neighborhood, but poor in the wonderful world of disposable income.

When June moved out and married the father of her baby (surprisingly, not the quarterback but rather the handsome young man who lived down the street), my father started to change. He was far less humorous, often came home late from work, and was more critical than ever of Chip. It was as if all his frustrations over June were manifesting themselves with his favorite whipping boy. There were constant criticisms of Chip and many bitter exchanges between the two. My mother was surprisingly silent through all these conflicts, almost afraid to provoke a worse situation. The rest of us were left wondering if our family was coming apart at the seams. Jaime withdrew even deeper into her own world of studying, very rarely even emerging to say goodnight. Pat and I wandered around the house trying to avoid the rooms where there were the most confrontations. Many a night I went to bed having to listen to Chip's tirade about what a miserable man our father was. It was during this time that I became quite adept at falling asleep surrounded by distracting noise and disruptive behavior. It was a trait that would serve me well the rest of my life.

The cornerstone of our family existence was always the nightly meal. The dining room was situated adjacent to the kitchen on one end and off the front foyer on the other. There were two entrances, both with swinging doors that blocked off the rest of the house. It was here that my father held forum. This was his bastion, his pulpit, where his rule and his voice were supreme. The two closed doors provided a captive audience. We were required to submit intelligent answers to his many questions and these answers had better be in the best of the Queen's English. I found out from listening to him that he was surprisingly versed in many areas of learning. An accountant by training, his knowledge of the English language, of literature, of history, and of current affairs was astounding. He wouldn't allow profanity in any fashion explaining that swearing was just a sign of ignorance because the one swearing couldn't think of a better word. He would quote Irish poets, challenge us with philosophical questions, and occasionally stump us with thought provoking riddles. I would dare say that I learned as much at supper time as I did most days at school. June's absence meant one empty chair at the table. It also meant that the harmony that had pervaded family dinners would be forever affected.

My father's business was doing very well in the late 1950's. American cars dominated the market and foreign competition was decades away. Chevrolet had a lineup of trendy cars and trucks. The 1955-1958 Chevy product was some of the most popular of all time. Life seemed to be good on Broad Street. My parents celebrated their economic windfall by hosting numerous parties. My father's only sister, Peg and her husband, Jim Anderson, quite possibly the funniest couple that ever lived, were frequent visitors. They shared a propensity for good times and alcohol. Add to the mix a colleague of my father, Don Child, who was a manager at GMAC, and his attractive, but usually intoxicated wife, Marge, and the good times were rolling. Pat and I would often hang around the kitchen and listen to the clink of highball glasses and the irreverent harmonies of the men drowned out by the high-pitched chorus of the women. It was usually time to leave the kitchen when Marge began to pinch my cheeks. She once woke me in the middle of the night to offer me a highball. I was twelve years old. On another occasion, Marge woke the whole house screeching that Don was missing. We all went scurrying about looking for Don. My father said he couldn't be too far away because he left his drink behind. It wasn't long before we found him. He had wandered out the back door, stumbled down the porch steps and was lying passed out in the blue spruce that bordered the driveway. In what continued to be a comedy of errors, my father and my uncle Jim were laughing hysterically while they tried to remove this 250 pound man from the bush and fell in unison into the same spruce. My aunt Peg capped the crazy episode by delivering a round of drinks on a tray to the "bushed" threesome who somehow managed to save some of their dignity by harmonizing "You're nobody 'til somebody loves you."

It was times like these when my father revealed a humorous side to his personality that he became most likable. It was also times like these when it was obvious that his affinity for alcohol had probably gone beyond recreational drinking and was being used to camouflage his broken heart. It was ironic that in these moments of intoxicated happiness, he seemed most vulnerable to his sobriety. Certainly his life had many blessings, but the disappointment of June's pregnancy had never vanished, not even when he sang with a high ball in his hand; for the longer he drank, the sadder the song.

# Chapter Four

## THE BIGGER STORY

WORKING AT NASA afforded me the opportunity of meeting and interacting with the most interesting people, from dedicated NASA scientists whose focus was conquering outer space, to star struck young secretaries whose focus was meeting their future soul mates. An average work day was never dull with endless projects that were always tagged with great urgency. I soon discovered that my job, as mundane as it originally seemed, was actually important. These brilliant scientists were generating fantastic volumes of journals and reports that required prompt editing from the editorial staff that was provided by the same contractor that employed me. From editorial, the reports were retyped in the technical typing pool by a team of extraordinarily competent typists. These girls could type pages of scientific data, including complicated graphs and formulas, by changing typing balls without missing a beat. This was the era before computers and spell check so their efficiency was mind boggling. I developed a healthy respect for these girls early on and their respect for my abilities became reciprocal when they delivered these journals and reports to my little corner of the operation with instructions that these manuscripts had to be copied, collated, stapled neatly and sent with the greatest speed to the mail room to be sent on the next plane to Washington, D.C. Mistakes at any stage of the process would not be tolerated. My part was certainly at the ground level but was, nonetheless, the part that produced the final product. In a weird sense, the lowest man on the totem pole was the one lastly responsible for its quality and appearance. My father's words: "any job worth doing is worth doing well," rang in my head every time the pressure was on. I became essential and that was very rewarding.

Each day, new people were finding their way into my area. From NASA executives to executive secretaries making three times what I made, there seemed to be a lineup of people who wanted to see and meet this new Xerox boy who was doing such a good job working with the editorial staff. Secretaries delivering work for me to do were hanging around longer and just chatting. Some were openly flirting and others were just satisfying their curiosity. I was the new kid on the block and I seemed to have a brain as well as the ability to collate hundreds of pages accurately and timely. In short, I was being checked out. My ego, still fragile from the dumping I received in college, was getting a much-needed boost. However, my radar was working overtime to make sure that a big rejection wasn't imminent. I was cautious of all the attention and consequently seemed aloof. To my great surprise, the more cautious I became, the more attention I seemed to receive. For someone from a small town with a population less than the occupants of this building the whole scenario seemed unreal. This was, after all NASA at its zenith, only two years removed from the first lunar landing on the moon. I wasn't in heaven yet, but I was rubbing elbows with people who knew all about the moon.

There was great excitement in the building every time there was a new launch. Work would stop and sixteen floors of employees would huddle around televisions to witness the next space adventure. The anticipation of an actual launch from Cape Canaveral was still a big deal and most people in the country would stop what they were doing and watch. There was great pride in NASA and consequently being associated with NASA, even just as a contractor, was exciting. It became even more exciting one day when two gentlemen in black suits came into my Xerox room and asked to see me. I couldn't imagine what reason these two had for wanting to see me. I soon found out that they were secret service and wanted to interview me for a secret clearance. They said it had come to their attention that I was being exposed to top-secret data and I had not yet been granted a secret clearance. They asked a barrage of questions, including a background check. They said the country was at war and there was a growing sympathy for the cause of the enemy. Specifically, they wanted my views on communism and student protest rights. Finally the questions settled on who I was, where I was from, who I associated with and who I lived with. I wondered at what point they were going to take me out back and shoot me. Of course, that never happened. They decided I was deserving of a top secret clearance, shook my hand, and left. If only they knew of some of Baxter's new friends from the bar, the firing squad might have been the approved option.

When I arrived at the apartment that night armed with the news of my new secret clearance, Baxter was also armed with some news of his own. Seated in our living room wearing a short mini-skirt and white thigh high boots was this striking brunette he introduced as Anna. I don't think anyone could prepare for Anna, and I was totally untutored. I could tell by the look on Baxter's face that he was enjoying the obviously awkward position his surprise guest had put me in. Here in the relative security of our less than immaculate apartment, and anticipating the chance to crash on the couch after an oppressively hectic day in the Xerox room, I suddenly had to recharge my energy and attempt to be polite and hopefully charming.

"Sean, this is Anna. She's a stewardess for TWA."

"Wow," I thought to myself.

"Nice to meet you, Anna. Welcome to Casa de Boys. This is quite a surprise. Usually Baxter only dates men, but I can see why he switched."

"Basster! Is this true? Are you just teasing me? I must be irresistible."

Not only was Anna stunning, she obviously had a sense of humor, and an unbelievably sexy Italian accent. In those first few minutes I realized that our lives as roommates were about to change and that Baxter was in for a hell of a ride. Suddenly, my secret service clearance didn't seem like such a big deal. Baxter had trumped that news in a big way.

# Chapter Five

## THE MAN WITH THE GOLDEN LEG

THE BOND BETWEEN Pat and I grew stronger as we entered our high school years. She still blamed me for chipping her tooth with a toy gun while I was chasing her around the ping pong table on roller skates when we were pre-teens. That was tempered by the knowledge that I knew of her occasional excursions out of the house beyond the dreaded curfew and had said nothing. She knew she could trust me. She also knew that I would attempt to defend her if her innocence was questioned or her reputation was being challenged. She was constantly telling guys, some of whom were quite scary, that they should be careful how they act or how they talked to her, or she would tell her brother. Physical confrontations were not my favorite, especially those with outcomes that were all too predictable, so I learned early in my high school days the art of confrontational bluffing and, if that approach failed, the art of diplomacy. With some well placed shouting as if angry and fortunately with the help of some of my football buddies, most possible altercations were cleverly avoided. Still, because I never backed down or appeared vulnerable, my reputation as being a defender of my sister allowed both Pat and I to position ourselves among the cool group. She became a cheerleader and I went on to play three sports. We were part of the 'in' crowd and life at school was sweet.

Pat started to date Gary during her junior year. Gary had moved to our town from the coal mining regions of Pennsylvania. His impact was immediate on the football team as he was quite

possibly the strongest and toughest player on the team. It bode
well for me that he and I were teammates and because he was
dating my sister, we formed a bond that nevertheless did not
preclude his squeezing my head with his massive arms until my
brain matter came out of my nose. It was my least favorite thing
about Gary but somehow I realized it was his way of showing
affection for his new little brother. He was gruff and unpolished
but he was basically a good guy—and having him around was sort
of like having a bodyguard. When I broke my wrist sophomore
year as the result of a dirty hit by an opposing player, it was Gary
who identified the perpetrator and revenged my injury by twisting
the guy's leg until he heard it snap. I grew to love the lunkhead
and as long as he treated my sister well, the terrifying thought of
having to defend her against Gary wouldn't be necessary.

At home, things were not as rosy. My father's devotion to his
beloved high balls had become a daily occurrence. He was using
my games as forums for his drunken escapades. My mother stop
coming to my games because she was humiliated by his actions.
The embarrassment he caused at these games made it difficult
for me to concentrate. His usual target was whatever official was
working that particular game. Baseball games were his favorites
because there were less people there. Consequently, his booming
voice could be heard all over the field. In one particular American
Legion baseball game in South Windsor, he became so vocal over
a call involving my tagging up too early from third base with the
potential winning run that he was led out of the ball field area by
police and told that if he ever returned, he would be put in jail.
Everyone on our team thought the whole incident was extremely
humorous; that is, everybody except me. I wasn't embarrassed
as much as I was angry. He was making my participation in
playing sports—something I loved doing my entire life—a living
nightmare. And it wasn't any better at home.

The supper hour, that pause in the daily grind that I always
looked forward to because it was the time for our family unit to
get together and share their stories of their day and it was my

mother's time to show off her great culinary skills, had become my
father's drunken show. Where once he had astounded us with his
knowledge, he now was confronting each of us with his alcohol-
induced speeches. June had gone to live with her new husband,
Rick, and her baby. Jaime was off to college, so only Chip, Pat and
I and my mother got to witness the nightly deterioration of my
father. For Chip, it was more of the same abuse to which he had
become accustomed, only much more personal. For Pat and me,
it was learning not to be confrontational because that would only
lead to an ugly scene. Mom sheepishly served the food and then
stepped back to her role of mediator. On days that my father came
home happy, we could count on familiar stories that were repeated
ad nauseam. One such story was of the man with the golden leg,
a story that I had once enjoyed as a kid. The story would climax
with my father bellowing: "Who stole my golden leg?" He would
wait until everyone was quiet, then slam his hand on the table and
point to one of us and yell "YOU DID!" He would then laugh
and leave the room. It was a very effective, funny story when we
were kids. Now, as young adults witnessing the fall of a great
man, the humor was gone.

# Chapter Six

## THE LOSS OF INNOCENCE

AT FIRST GLANCE, Baxter and Anna seemed perfect for each other. They were about the same height and weight; both had dark features, a year round tan and shared a passion for looking in the mirror. They had met at Baxter's bar when Anna took a second job as a waitress in between international flights. She was confident, pretty, and beguiling. She was also eight years older than Baxter. The eight-year difference made Anna more worldly, more mysterious, wiser in the ways of the city, and more capable of controlling the relationship. Baxter, however, was a good foil for Anna because being devious or sometimes on the edge of honorable, were traits that were part of Baxter's personality even before he had moved to Boston. The two of them became not only lovers but also partners—partners in some shady schemes that involved their employment at the bar.

My usual day, which often included hours of overtime, generally ended with a trip to the bar for a bite to eat and a couple of beers. Anna always made a big deal of my being there and, of course, Baxter welcomed the chance to come back to earth and talk to someone who knew where he was coming from and knew where he was going. The bar was filled with regulars, true characters who gave the place a personality, however sordid. It was the precursor to CHEERS, where everyone knew your name. The big difference was everyone in this bar knew mostly aliases, because this place was frequented by some of Boston's most notorious.

"Hey, Big Al, how's it hanging?"

"Hanging low and loose," Al responded. "Maybe this little luscious thing would like to straighten it out." Anna had just served Al a glass of his favorite Merlot.

Big Al Campbonelli was a prototypical Italian boy from the North End of Boston. He frequented the bar in the late afternoons to brag about his previous night's activities and to connect with various patrons of the bar who would find a corner to discuss their business. He was tall, handsome, and obviously quite sold on himself. From my frequent appearances at the bar, I had become someone to whom Big Al liked to brag. Although physically imposing and despite the appearance of self-assuredness, Al still lived in his parent's house. This fact alone drew Al to Baxter and me because Al was fascinated with the fact that we had our own apartment. When Al found out that Anna lived with us, he became a nuisance. He was constantly inviting himself over to our place and we were constantly finding excuses not to let that happen. It was better to keep Al as a bar acquaintance. Our home was our castle and we didn't need some Italian stud storming our walls looking to become a non-paying roommate. We came to Boston without a clue, but our developing street sense was becoming keen to possible dangers.

One day I became brave after several Jack Daniels, my newly acquired friend, and I asked Al what he did for a living. His answer was quick and succinct.

"Imports! Exports!"

"What do you import, Al? And what do you export?"

"That's not for you to know, Sean. I wouldn't want to have to...you know the saying!" I indeed knew the saying and although I imagined him to be harmless, I knew enough to keep Al at a safe distance.

At the far end of the bar sat a very big, quiet gentleman who always dressed in black. He looked up momentarily when Al was being his macho self. He quickly caught Baxter's eye and then glanced back to his drink. The man in black was there most days. He would then disappear for a couple of weeks. His return was always unnoticed as he very much kept to himself. He would engage in soft conversation with Baxter whom he seemed to really like. Baxter had that way of getting people to trust him and tell him their life's story. The man in black obviously had a story to tell and I was curious to know what it was. I was smart enough, however, to wait until we were home in our apartment, where no one could hear his answer, to ask my roommate about the man in black. Baxter told me his name, at least the one he used in the bar, was Bob Black.

"He's a hit man. He kills people for a living."

I was glad I had waited to ask Baxter because my mouth stayed open for several minutes while I digested this little bit of news.

"You are kidding me, right." I finally said.

"No! He's a hit man. I don't know why he confided in me, but don't ever let on that you know or he'll take it out on me. He thinks it's funny the way Big Al tries to act the role of a tough guy. He said someday maybe he'd show him what a tough guy is really like."

What a bar! There was Big Al who wanted everybody to think he was somebody to be feared and then there was Bob Black who didn't want anybody to know what he did because he was a professional killer. I had to find a new place to drink.

Anna had moved in with us the previous week. The apartment was plenty big so I didn't think things would change that much. Initially, her move was uneventful, but gradually I was beginning to feel like the third wheel. She was extremely demanding of Baxter, constantly reminding him that if he wanted some, he had better keep her happy, and keeping her happy meant giving up his soul. Baxter, for a time, thought he was playing her, but it was evident to me that the puppet was Baxter and Anna was pulling the strings. It became increasingly difficult for the two of us to hang around like the old days, bar hopping to places like the "Point After", the sports bar owned by Gino Cappelletti, who played for the New England Patriots. Whenever Baxter wanted to do something, Anna would always impose her will. I wasn't jealous of the relationship, or even envious, but I missed our time together because we were buddies who had jointly embarked on this great Boston adventure. What's worse is that whenever I had an invited guest over to the apartment, Anna would go into her Queen Bee act and intimate that she and I had something going on. Her interference in my nonexistent social life was putting a major damper on our relationship. I found her beautiful and charming, but also mettlesome and annoying. We were both strong willed people and it was just a matter of time before we butted heads.

That time came soon enough when after months of attempting a reconciliation with my ex-girlfriend, Alix, the one who had dumped me on graduation day at college, I had convinced her to come over for dinner. I had planned to cook the only thing I knew how to—steak and French fries, with a salad. I picked a night when Baxter was working and Anna was on a flight. I had aspirations of a great evening where we would rekindle our fractured relationship. Initially, the evening went along smoothly with some light conversation and some wine. It was great to see her and I could sense that she too was ready to possibly forgive me for my college indiscretion. The meal turned out surprisingly well. She loved the apartment. She was beginning to laugh and enjoy herself and suddenly all the old feelings were coming back. And then we could hear a key in the door.

It was Anna. Her flight had been cancelled and she came home early. I had not explained to Alix that I had a female roommate because I didn't feel it was relevant. She knew Baxter but had no idea that Anna was a third roommate. Her countenance immediately changed. Anna was stunning in her TWA uniform and she immediately went into her routines. Even though I explained to Alix that Anna was Baxter's girl, Anna felt compelled to imply that something was also going on between us. I could see the joy drain out of Alix's face as Anna openly flirted with me, something she never did when we were alone. She was in her element and the performance sapped the life out of the evening.

"Sean, have you told your girlfriend how much fun the three of us have?"

Sensing the night was over, I stood up to attempt to talk to Anna, to explain that this wasn't just any girl; this was the one girl that meant something to me. Before I could say anything, Anna put her arms around me and gave me a big kiss. She then made sure Alix saw her grab my ass and say coyly, "I'll leave you two alone now. Don't do anything I wouldn't do."

Alix didn't say much on the way home. It was fruitless to try to explain Anna because I'm sure she had never met anyone like her. One thing was for sure; the reconciliation was over.

After the Alix-Anna debacle, I welcomed the chance to go away for the weekend to a National Guard drill in Connecticut. I was furious with Anna but as the weekend went on, I gradually calmed down and realized she was just being herself. It was my fault that I hadn't warned Alix about her. It was May of 1970 and the papers were full of pictures of four dead students on the campus of Kent State who, while protesting the war in Vietnam, had been shot dead by nervous and undisciplined National Guard soldiers sent to quell the riot. Our weekend drill took on a whole new significance. We were no longer being trained in combat for possible deployment to Vietnam, but were now being trained in riot control for possible deployment on our nation's college campuses. It was an unsettled time. Robert Kennedy was assassinated in 1968 in Los Angeles and Martin Luther King was shot down by an assassin two months earlier in Memphis. In anger, blacks were burning down inner cities and students were protesting an unpopular war. It all made my little problem with Anna pale in comparison.

I drove back to Boston on Sunday evening after the drill, still wearing my National Guard fatigues. With my uniform on and my hair short, it all seemed too obvious what side I was on in the protest issue. My true feelings became apparent when I reached Boston and was attempting to park my car in front of our apartment. A policeman came running up to me and asked what I was doing on the street. I answered that I was coming back from a weekend Guard drill and lived in the apartment across the street. He told me to get inside and stay there. He didn't give me an explanation. I went inside the apartment. Baxter and Anna were eating pizza and drinking wine. I asked them what was going on and they had no idea. I told them about the policeman and we all went to the big window facing the street to try to find out what the problem was. We looked down the avenue to our right. There on the edge of Mass Ave. were about a hundred policemen in full riot gear. Northeastern University was just around the corner in the opposite direction from the police. We could hear chanting in the distance getting louder as a crowd approached. From their campus on Huntington Avenue, hundreds of students marched up Hemenway Street along the Fenway and gathered at the beginning of our street, facing the police. The students pushed forward chanting "We shall overcome" while the police advanced in riot formation. We couldn't believe that this was all happening right in front of our apartment. Both sides stopped about a hundred feet apart with the police warning the protesters with a bullhorn to disperse and go back to their campus. The students continued to chant and some of the more aggressive ones shouted obscenities and threw eggs at the police. What then transpired was a sign of the times that were unsettled and violent. The police charged at the students striking many with their clubs. Students were scampering for cover and some were being run down and beaten. In spite of our own riot training, our allegiance was to the students. We emptied our refrigerator of all the eggs we had and began to throw them at the police from our fourth floor window. It had little effect other than to make us feel better. Many students were hurt and beaten that night; many were arrested. But for the three of us the images that were laid out in front of us of police brutality and complete disregard for human life left an indescribable picture of a society gone mad. Life in Boston would forever be affected by those images.

# Chapter Seven

## THE JOURNEY TO HELL

IN THE 60'S, alcoholism was thought of as a weakness, not the perverse disease that was identified by doctors years later. In the advanced stages the affliction brought with it many side effects. Most often it took years of regular abuse to slide into the abyss of alcoholism. Bizarre behavior, a total disregard for rules or laws of society, and an absolute refusal to admit that there was a problem, were symptoms that were commonplace and telltale to its presence. It was a quiet assassin that snuck up on unsuspecting souls and rendered them incoherent and incapable of dealing with day to day life. Unlike today's revelations of the disease and its origins, victims of its addiction were ostracized and ridiculed for not having the will power to combat the condition.

The times were ripe with excess. The economy was booming. Social clubs such as the Elks and the American Legion were prevalent in most towns. Most of these clubs offered drinks at discount prices and encouraged their members to engage in social drinking in a protected, secretive environment. If a spouse of a member called to find out the whereabouts of their husband, they were met with a set answer of "I don't believe he's here right now but I'll give him the message if I see him." Most often that message was fodder for a good laugh at the bar. These men's only clubs had the intention of providing a haven for their members to escape from outside realities. In some cases, the heavy drinking to forget their problems became the reality.

Many alcoholics were also heavy smokers; many gambled heavily; and most drove their cars on roads and highways without a second thought of legal or moral consequences. If a drunken driver were stopped for erratic driving in those days, they were often told to go home and sleep it off by policemen who were part of the good old boys' network. Most people believed that if the alcoholic was left alone, they would eventually stop drinking and everything would go back to normal.

My father was the classic alcoholic in every sense. When he would start his binge drinking, he would transform himself from the responsible family man and business owner to a gregarious and an offensive drunk. He smoked three to four packs of Chesterfields every day; he drank Schenley and Seagrams whiskey excessively on a daily basis; and he loved to play poker with his drinking pals at the Elks Club. These barracudas, who pretended to be his best friends, were more than happy to take his money that came from the dealership receipts that he quite often forgot to deposit in the bank on his way home. He literally became another person, one who could be counted on by his pals to throw his money around like it was water, but who couldn't be counted on by his family to show up for supper on time or sober. When he did eventually come home, he was verbally abusive, especially to poor Chip, who never could escape being the object of my father's wrath. The more time went by, the more he drank; and the more he drank, the more bizarre became his behavior.

One night after Chip and I had gone to bed and were fast asleep, there suddenly was a loud noise in the hallway outside our room. Our bedroom door was thrown open and in the shadows of the doorway stood our father with a baseball bat in his hand ranting about getting rid of the intruders who were in the room. Somehow, he had imagined burglars had entered the house while he was passed out downstairs in his chair. In his mind he saw Chip and I as the burglars and he was going to chase us out of the house with the bat. He raised the bat to swing it at Chip when my mother stepped in followed by June's husband, Rick, whom my mother had called to come over to help. They managed to disarm my father and we were told to go back to sleep. Of course, sleep didn't come easily for either one of us. The next morning, nothing was said at the breakfast table about the previous night's incident. Consequently, one more recollection of our happy childhood was entered into our memory bank.

The following weeks and months saw a further decline in my father's behavior. It was as if he were haunted by demons. He suffered through a spell of hiccups that lasted for days into weeks. The doctors were baffled by his condition but seemingly couldn't find a cure. They warned him to no avail that if he didn't stop drinking, he would face serious health consequences. But classically, he denied he had a problem, although the constant hiccupping had to have been driving him even crazier by the day. The final straw came one afternoon while I was studying in our living room with a friend. My father came home inebriated and proceeded to warn us about the rodents that he spotted running up the wall next to the fireplace. He then spent the next few minutes attempting to pick them off the wall with his bare hands. My friend looked at me in disbelief for there were no rodents there and, indeed, my father was picking at the air. In his stupor, he was vividly imagining the rodents and was doing his best to rid us of the problem. He was suffering from what was later described to me as the delirious tremors or DT's, a condition that often afflicts those with an advanced case of alcoholism. My father had reached the end of a very rocky trip and something had to be done.

That night an intervention of sorts happened at our house. My mother had summoned June and Rick, and Pat's boyfriend, Gary. Both Rick and Gary were good sized individuals and Chip and I joined them in convincing my father that he had to have drastic treatment and it had to be done right away. Of course he denied he had a problem, but there would be no negotiations this evening. It was decided that Rick and Gary, along with my mother, would drive my father to a rehab facility in Westerly, Rhode Island, about an hour away. The doctor who ran the clinic had some success in treating alcoholics and my father was in desperate need. That night was the last time I saw my father for several weeks. I prayed that when he came back, he would be the man I had idolized as a kid.

Looking back I could remember many of the qualities that had made my father the person that he was—the man that had been my role model. He always seemed bigger than he actually was. He stood only about five feet seven inches and weighed less than a hundred and fifty pounds, but his stature in the community and the way he related to the town's people always impressed me. He seemed to know everybody by their first name and everyone knew him. Sure he was tight with a dollar when it came to business, but his donations to local charities were well known. Tales told to me by my Aunt Peg of his athletic accomplishments always fascinated me. It was said that as a boy growing up in Manchester, Connecticut, a suburb just east of Hartford, he was the most gifted swimming and diving athlete to come from that area. His prowess as a diver led to his earning a scholarship to Boston University from which he graduated in 1933. Indeed, the family trophy case was filled with trophies and ribbons from his days at B.U. According to my mother's accounts, he was also a bit of a daredevil. Once when they were courting, they stopped at a roadside scenic overlook that jutted out over a steep valley below. The overlook was protected by an iron railing to keep people from falling. My father decided to impress my mother by doing a handstand on the railing. It was a foolish gesture but nonetheless won for him a kiss from my mother. She always glowed when she told that story. He also co-owned a small engine plane and regularly skimmed the tree tops for the thrill of it. That phase of his life ended when the other owner of the plane crashed in the woods and was killed. Dad took his death hard and never flew again.

When Pat and I were small, he would impress our friends with a diving trick. He had installed a diving board at the end of the dock at our summer cottage on nearby Alexander's lake.

When he came home from work, our friends would beg him to do his dive. He would first light a cigarette then approach the board. He would then throw a quarter into the deeper water at the end of the dock. Next came an absolutely perfect jackknife dive performed with the cigarette still lit in his mouth. He would stay down underwater for what seemed like an eternity, and then surface with the cigarette still lit and the quarter in his hand. Our friends were astonished and we were proud that he was our Dad. He seemed invincible.

Years of drinking had changed that hero who had amazed us with his dive. To see my father at his worst in his battle with the bottle left me disillusioned and deflated. My Dad had flaws in his personality that to me were difficult to fathom. I was fourteen years old and I was being exposed to an unfortunate adult reality. I didn't handle these revelations very well.

# Chapter Eight

## UP! UP! AND AWAY!

MY RISE THROUGH the ranks at NASA was surprisingly mercurial. From literally the depths of the operation (the Xerox room in the bowels of the building), promotions were coming fast. With the added responsibilities, came more hours and more hours meant less time to play. Unfortunately for me, my elevation upstairs to the editorial floor was not accompanied by the expected raise in pay. Thanks to our beloved President Nixon, there was a freeze on hourly wages that was an unsuccessful attempt to curb rising inflation. I could have been promoted to the director of NASA and I still would have been paid the entry level salary that I was given when I started as the copy making stooge in the basement. My first promotion was a jump from the ground floor to the photo lab where I spent all the sunny hours buried in the dark room. The job was fascinating. I learned the process of taking a photo and developing it in chemicals that had the smell of toxins and the ingredients to defoliate my soft cushy hands and turn them into the skin of an Iguana. I learned that secretaries, usually the lower tiered ones with not a great deal to lose, loved to visit the darkroom where my coworker, a red neck from Tennessee, and I would roll out the red carpet and practice our photography. I also learned that supervisors absolutely shunned the area for fear of soiling their fifty dollar sports jackets and their patent leather shoes. And I learned that working late hours left only enough time to go directly to the bars. When those evenings went deep into the night, the dark room was a convenient place to roll up and sleep and wake up the next morning in the same clothes as the previous day, a fact very few people even noticed or cared about. It was pretty much carte blanche in the photo lab as long as you did good work in a timely manner.

My time in the lab lasted only a few months. One day, I was asked to fill in for a chronically absent proof reader in the editorial office. The editor in charge was a crusty old World War II veteran named Frank Lynn. He was brilliant and cantankerous, charmingly witty and pugnacious, and opinionated, very opinionated. Frank was a Harvard grad but he was more proud of his days serving as a first lieutenant under General George Patton in World War II. Frank was notoriously tough on his assistants, but from day one we struck up a friendship and a camaraderie that was to lead to a fantastic working relationship. In many ways, I saw Frank as an extension of my father. He had the same proud Irish heritage, was educated in Boston, had a great sense of humor along with a rapier intellect, liked his Irish whiskey, and was at the ready to stand up for his principles.

That first day in editorial was chaotic but exciting. Frank and I were to proofread and edit several top secret documents and rewrite the brilliant but poorly written reports into understandable English. We were dealing with scientific experiments from some of the top NASA scientists. Just being a part of this history-making period of time was scintillating. We not only accomplished the task, we did so with time to spare. The reports went to Washington on a plane that night and the director himself applauded our work. Frank was beaming with pride on our accomplishment and was very quick to ask my superior to immediately assign me to his office on a permanent basis. His wish was granted and I was now the number two man on the editorial floor. I had bypassed my immediate supervisor, and I was now the intermediary between our office and the secretarial pool. I was even in charge of my Tennessee cohort in the photo lab. My status in the group of editorial contractors had taken a colossal leap. Everything at work was going spectacularly well—everything except President Nixon's wage freeze.

Because of my new responsibilities at work, it was becoming rare for me to be in the apartment with either Baxter or Anna. They also were busy working and, of course, playing together. It was somewhat disconcerting to me that with all the success I was enjoying at work, Baxter was the one that always had the big wad of money on him and the big smile on his face. Life was treating Baxter well. He had become a bit of a celebrity in the night club scene and was dating an Italian bombshell. I'm certainly not petty enough to begrudge Baxter his success but I did envy the disposable income that for me was frozen. Nixon hadn't yet figured out how to freeze bartenders incomes. But then, the balloon burst.

Baxter came home and announced: " I have to find another job. They've been watching Anna and me at work and they think we've been dipping into the company profits."

Anna interrupted with another of her astute remarks. "Basster got caught with his hands in the cookie jar, Sean. I told him we were being watched and he didn't believe me. It's all his fault."

Somehow I doubted her innocence. Here's what I knew. Anna was a fashion horse, always wearing expensive designer clothes. They were frequenting high class restaurants and were planning a vacation to the Bahamas. I was eating at Burger King on a regular basis and was generally trying to figure out how to get to the next payday without going into a big hole. Our lease was coming due and the landlord was threatening a large increase in rent. Our first year in Boston had certainly not been without excitement but unless something changed drastically, our big adventure was going to end after one year.

# Chapter Nine

## THE LAW OF DIMINISHING RETURNS

IT WAS A summer to remember. My lifelong friends and I made the most of our last days together before we split in a hundred different directions. It was a crazy, carefree time when you could just enjoy your buddies and not worry about embarrassing yourself or disgracing your school. We were high school graduates now and we felt free to spread our wings and literally fly into the future. It was during that summer most of us learned how to drink. How much to drink took us a little longer to figure out. Even though it was years before society cracked down on teenage drinking, we actually showed that for the most part we were responsible. We didn't drive around once we started to drink; we usually stayed wherever we were until it was time to go home. The guys who were driving cars would drink modestly. It was an indication that we cared for each other and watched each other's backs.

We had our preferred places to drink, spots that were off the beaten track. Our favorite spot was called the sand banks, which was down a dark, sparsely traveled country road. The sand banks were used in the winter to provide sand for snow covered roads and in the summer they were the perfect amphitheater for our parties. Older friends would buy the beer and off we'd go to laugh, to remember, and to harmonize to our favorite songs blaring from the car radios. One night as I sang "Graduation Day" by the Beach Boys with my friends, Dennis, Ricky, Charlie, and Bob, I thought of the great joy I saw on my father's face whenever he would sing with his friends. I realized then that I wasn't all that different from my father. I was sure that at my age he shared similar nights with his buddies. I wondered how it all went wrong for him, how drinking had gotten the best of him. I promised myself that I would never let that happen to me.

As the summer wound down, the day came to depart for college. To describe my life to this point as sublime would not be descriptive enough to portray a beautiful time in a beautiful place. My father's battle with his Irish demons notwithstanding, the time spent growing up in Connecticut during the 50's and early 60's was a snapshot of a simpler life. The air seemed cleaner. The sky and the water in the lakes and rivers seemed bluer. The grass, of course, seemed greener. Friends were genuine without ulterior motives. Families were bonded by a love for one another and a devotion to their church, their school, and their businesses. Kids and the elderly could walk the streets without fear and the problems of society were confined to the big cities. It was quite simply the age of innocence.

As a family, we gathered on that Sunday in the fall of 1964 to celebrate and to reminisce. Mom outdid herself and prepared a huge roast beef dinner. Everyone was there: June and Rick, who now had three boys; Jaime, who was teaching high school and living in the neighboring town of Woodstock; Chip, who, ironically, was working for my father in his parts department and still living at home; and Pat, who was working for the town as a secretary and still going hot and heavy with Gary. The dogs, Clipper and Jeff, our brother-sister beagles were wandering around as if they were about to lose their best friend. I loved these family functions and I loved my family, but I sensed that I was about to break away from their security blanket and embark on a world of new adventures. I was happy and sad at the same time. Like a microcosm of my life, this celebration was going to end.

When I went to my room to pack my bag, the realization hit me that my room was never going to be my room anymore. Sure, I would be visiting on weekends and summer vacations; but from then on, I would belong to another address in another place. I knew college was going to be an exciting experience. I was certain that my new life would be filled with rewarding achievements in the pursuit of knowledge and that I was preparing myself for a future career wherever that may be. I convinced myself that I would soon be making new friends and that my old friends would remain close forever. With all these assurances, it was nonetheless difficult to hide the tears in my eyes as I got into the car to drive off to school. Backing the car out of that familiar driveway, away from the familiar house that I grew up in and the less than perfect family that I was leaving behind, made me realize what a great life I had up until this point. I knew I could come back as often as I wanted and I knew that I would always be welcomed; but I also knew that as the years stretched long down uncertain roads, my visits would be less and less frequent. I suddenly realized that I was driving into the future, another victim of the law of diminishing returns.

# Chapter Ten

## OUTWARD BOUND

IT DIDN'T TAKE Baxter and Anna long to find work in a new bar. Baxter, despite his indiscretions, was as good a bartender as there was in the city. One look at Anna and any owner wanting to attract young men to their bar, would hire her on the spot and without references. Their new jobs, however, didn't justify our paying the rather large increase in rent our landlord had imposed on our Fenway apartment. We decided to look around for another rental. A friend told us about a new complex in the Brighton area of Boston, and that weekend we went to look. The location was right on a pond with a large grass field separating the water from the three buildings which made up a triangle. Baxter and I were always doing something athletic so the thought of having a field right outside our door was a great attraction. The apartment we looked at was quite a bit smaller than our previous one, but it was brand new with two bedrooms and a deck. Without any further investigating, we signed a lease and moved in the next week. What we didn't know was that our new location just outside the city, the Chandler Pond Apartments, was inhabited with mostly young professionals or students from wealthy backgrounds who were attending either Boston College or Boston University. BC was only two blocks away on the other side of the pond and BU was a couple of MBTA stops down Commonwealth Avenue. We had luckily stumbled into a hotbed of young people, a high percentage of whom seemed quite interesting. In addition, a larger group of apartments adjacent to ours, called Town Estates, provided an even greater mix of young people. We were giddy with our new surroundings. It was city living in a breeding area.

We thought our last address had been ideal because of its location and close proximity to the downtown hotspots. The drawbacks, however, were also palpable and numerous. Crime was a neighbor that reared its ugly head on a regular basis. Apartments, including ours, were frequently broken into by pushers and potheads looking for valuables to support their habits. During the warm months, prostitutes camped out on our front steps on such a regular basis that we got to know many of them on a first name basis. Baxter and I would even bring them coffee on some cold nights just to be hospitable. It became less than ideal when you would come back to your apartment with a date and have several girls of the night address you by your first name. Add to the scene some pimps, some addicts, an occasional fight, police sirens, an unhealthy dose of drunken bums, and the incessant blaring of multi-cultural music wafting out of a hundred different windows; and you could imagine the growing discontent we had with our neighborhood. When the rent went up, our decision to move was an easy one. After gathering our meager belongings, we stuffed them into my 1971 Ford Pinto, and took off for the greener pastures of Brighton. The drive only took about ten minutes without traffic, but the difference in all aspects of our new address was positive. We had found an oasis, complete with our own parking spaces, just minutes from downtown. No more dealing with the complexities of inner city living. No more fear of being robbed or mugged or worse. No more trying to find a parking place on opposite sides of the street on alternate days. No more drama, and as I was to soon find out, no more living with Anna.

# Chapter Eleven

## THERE WAS NO PLACE LIKE HOME

IT IS SAID that absence makes the heart grow fonder. My first few months at college proved to be a reinforcement of that classic line. For the first time in my cloistered little life, I was the outsider. When I decided to go to college out of state, Merrimack College seemed to be the perfect choice. It was situated in North Andover, Massachusetts which was less than a hundred miles from my home, although it seemed like it was a million miles away. Merrimack had been founded by Cardinal Cushing of Boston in 1947 to accommodate the growing numbers of Catholic students that were graduating from Boston area high schools. And therein posed the problem. Everyone in every class seemed to know each other. It didn't help that I was basically shy and incapable of finding common ground with a room full of strangers. The first couple of weeks were excruciating. It was like I didn't exist. To make matters worse, my three roommates in the dormitory were pathologically strange. Jack, the most talkative, spent most of his time popping pimples in the mirror. George, a little squirrelly guy, laughed out loud at nothing and had a weird look in his eyes like he might have been a serial killer. Bob was from Maine. He looked like a cartoon character and was trying out for Commodore of the sailing team. None of the three had ever played sports although George said he had once blown up a car at his high school during a pep rally. I couldn't believe I was going to be living with these three for the whole year. I thought about home often and wondered if I should have gone to the University of Connecticut with most of my friends.

During orientation, the committee asked for anybody with a football background to sign up for the freshman team that would be playing the sophomores in game of touch football. I raised my hand, thankful for the opportunity to get away from my roommates for awhile. During tryouts I met some normal guys who shared my passion for sports. Even though it was only touch football, we gave that sophomore team a serious beating. I couldn't believe the crowd that was at the game. The entire freshman class and most of the sophomore class were there. I had a very good game playing wide receiver and defensive back and because of the notoriety of that performance, people were suddenly talking to me in class. It was amazing how friendly everybody had become. All my life to this point, sports had been the catalyst for a lot of great memories involving a lot of great friends. When my spirit was at its lowest point, lost in the uncertainty of whether or not I had chosen the right college, sports once again had been the link between being considered an outsider or being accepted. Now, I thought to myself, if I could only spend as little time as possible in the dorm with my wacky roommates, life at Merrimack would be a great deal more interesting.

The library proved to be the safe haven I was seeking my freshman year. There was something very consoling about being surrounded by hundreds of books that contained the works of the world's greatest minds. I could do the homework required for my courses in the quiet of the library among other students who were similarly motivated to succeed. My favorite high school teacher, Mr. Brine, had challenged my dedication by telling me I wouldn't last a week in college if I continued to put sports and social life ahead of academics. I took the challenge personally, determined to prove Mr. Brine wrong. I was also motivated by the fear of my father's wrath if I came home with lousy grades. When I made the Dean's List at the end of the marking period, I made sure Mr. Brine knew. I could tell by his reaction that his challenge was meant to be motivational and that he was proud of me. My father's reaction was all too predictable. He just said: "Good! That's what you're there for".

I spent a great deal of time that first semester just thinking about my family when I was taking breaks from studying at the library. I realized how fortunate I was to have a family like mine. In particular, I missed my mother. I missed her laughter and I missed her cooking; but most of all, I just missed her presence. It always seemed that in her eyes I could do no wrong. It's a trait I would later be looking for in a wife.

# *Chapter Twelve*

## THE QUEEN BEE LEAVES THE HIVE

ALTHOUGH ANNA WAS in favor of moving to the new location, it wasn't long before she became apprehensive of the lifestyle upon which she was about to embark. She felt like she was moving to the country. She never bothered to get her driver's license and relied on Baxter to take her everywhere. Her infrequent overseas flights were generally at night so while living in town, late night trips to Logan Airport were not that inconvenient for Baxter. When he was tied up at work, they both knew they could ask me to give her a ride for I was never too sorry to see Anna leave —if only for a little while.Anna knew how to get around in the city. She knew the subways and the bus routes and she knew she could always rely on her obvious charm to solicit a ride from a bar patron or a local neighbor. She was supremely gifted in the art of seductive manipulation and used her gift to garner many favors. Life in Brighton offered a whole new set of hurdles to which she was unaccustomed. The grocery store was over a mile away. Her job in her new bar was many stops down the subway line and the bar closed after the trains stopped for the night. Her friends from her old neighborhood were scattered about the city and many had moved to new addresses. The biggest hurdle, however, was the competition that came with the territory. If Anna was one thing, it was territorial. She was used to being the Queen Bee. She had always been the best looking, the best dressed, the sexiest—the center of attention. At Chandler Pond, Anna wasn't even the best looking stewardess.

Dale and Maureen, two American Airline stews moved into the basement apartment right below our first floor corner unit on the same day we arrived. They were the first of the many new neighbors we were to meet that day, the first day of the new lease. They were down to earth, friendly, and gorgeous. None of these traits set well with Anna. She pouted most of that first day. The next day proved to be even worse for Anna as a number of attractive young ladies moved into the adjoining apartments. The "piece de resistance" came when a Doris Day look-a-like, a lovely young blond, moved into the unit directly across from our deck, just a few yards past the path separating the buildings. When she asked Baxter and I to give her a hand carrying in her belongings, I thought Anna was going to freak. When we returned with smiles on our faces and a plate of freshly baked cookies, she did freak.

"Basster, I cant' believe you. You're acting like a horny teenager. How can you even look at another girl when you have me? And Sean, you're nothing but a bad influence on Basster. The two of you need your dicks cut off."

In spite of the graphic reference to our private parts, my hopeful radar was working overtime. Anna continued to yell at Baxter and accused him of being a gigolo. She stormed out the door only to return in a few minutes demanding a ride to a girlfriend's house. He probably shouldn't have, but Baxter laughed at her and told her she was being ridiculous. However, there was no consoling Anna on this day. Her reign as the center of Baxter's world was coming to an end, and she knew it.

# Chapter Thirteen

## THE ROAD TO UNDERSTANDING

DURING MY FRESHMAN year, I came home at least once a month. My mother would welcome me with my favorite meal of swordfish grilling in the stove. As I turned into the driveway, my senses of taste and smell would activate as if on a sensor system. Mom's meals never disappointed. She could have been a chef in a five-star restaurant. Her cooking was legendary, at least in my mind. It's amazing how quickly you can adapt to mediocre food when you eat all your meals in a cafeteria. You eat because you need fuel to study and what you eat doesn't seem to matter. There's almost no taste, just volume. It doesn't take long to miss the wonderful home-cooked meals of your mother, and the longer you're away, the greater the memories of what good food really tastes like.

My visits home would be something of an event in our house. Everyone, from my siblings to their children to friends I hadn't seen for awhile, would be there to greet me and listen to my stories of college life and my tales of my crazy roommates. The stress of succeeding in college seemed to disappear when I was in the friendly confines of home. The weekend was always too short and before long, I was packing a doggy bag full of goodies, my fresh smelling, clean laundry that my mother was nice enough to do for me, and whatever books I had brought home and failed to open. Leaving at the end of the weekend was as Shakespeare wrote, "sweet sorrow" for it was another goodbye in a succession of goodbyes.

Sophomore and Junior years were different. As I became more involved with life at school, my visits became fewer and fewer. I joined a fraternity my sophomore year; I ran for Junior Class president and was elected; and I met Alix. My main focus was now at school and visits home were rare. In the summer, my schedule centered on playing baseball seven days a week in a semi-pro league. The games always included a nightly stop at the bar that sponsored our team to replay the game with my teammates until closing. Even though I was home, I was seldom at the house except to sleep.

I guess it's inevitable to seek independence at some age. It was becoming increasingly evident that my late nights with the team were becoming a problem for my parents. They didn't approve of this new swashbuckling lifestyle. They very rarely saw me although they knew from my sleeping late in the morning that I had been out late the night before. They worried about my safety and were concerned that I was heading for a train wreck. I think they were happy when I went back to school.

In the spring of my junior year, my mother called with an unusual request. My father's bookkeeper had taken an extended leave of absence due to illness and my mother had taken over the job temporarily. She was calling to ask if I would help her in the office for the summer. She said she could use the help and it would be a way she could keep her eye on me. I knew that the last part of the request was tongue in cheek, a reference to my behavior the previous summer, but I accepted with a little trepidation. I didn't like the car business and I wanted her to know this was something I was only going to do once.

My father's dealership had always been considered by Chevrolet as one of its 'Mom and Pop stores'. It was one of the smallest dealerships in his zone. He seemed to be successful in his operation and he seemed to be making decent money, but this was an era of growth at Chevrolet and his factory representative was constantly after him to build a new facility in a new area of town. They wanted a showcase dealership not a converted gas station with apartments upstairs. Knowing how much my father valued his money, a new facility probably wouldn't be something he was going to do anytime soon.

The last few years had been a struggle for my father. After several relapses into his old drinking habits, he seemed to have finally defeated his demons. However, a routine check of his chronic coughing, a direct result of years of heavy smoking, uncovered a cancerous growth in his mouth. He had to quit smoking, which he did; and he had to undergo a barrage of radiation treatments to try to kill the cancer cells. The closest facility with radiation capabilities was at Hartford Hospital, 50 miles away. What my mother hadn't told me about my summer job was that it was going to be my responsibility to drive my father to Hartford every day for his treatments. I later found out that my father had requested that I be the one to drive him.

School ended and I went home to assume my new position of assistant bookkeeper and chauffeur for my father. I wondered how he and I would be able to hold a conversation during these hour-long trips. In my whole life we probably never had a conversation that lasted more than a few minutes. It's funny how things turn out.

I had never considered my father to be just a regular guy. I had no idea that he had fears and concerns like everyone else. I guess I always saw him as some sort of Superman, indestructible and fearless, and I had never known him to be sentimental. All those impressions changed over the next few weeks. I had the opportunity to really get to know him on these drives to Hartford. Fate sometimes puts us where we least expect to be but there was no doubt that I was meant to be with my father during these challenging times. The sentimental side came out one day when we were traveling through his hometown of Manchester where he grew up. He asked me to go a different way that day so he could see some familiar landmarks in town. As we drove down a side road, he told me to stop the car for a minute. I recognized the house. It was the house where the Andersons had lived. His beloved sister, Peg, my favorite aunt, had passed away from breast cancer a couple of years earlier and the family had since sold the house. As he sat there slumped over, his eyes filled with tears and before long we were both crying. He said through his tears: "She was a great gal. God took her way too early. I don't think I'll ever get over her death." He repeated, "She was a great gal." We sat there for a few more minutes until I told him that we had to go to make his appointment. The rest of the drive was quiet. On the way home from the hospital, the only words he spoke were: "Love your sisters. You just never know." Unfortunately, his words were very prophetic.

## Chapter Fourteen

### FROM BAZAAR TO SUBLIME

FOR ME, OUR move to Brighton was a perfect one. Although I had acclimated quite nicely to the role of a city slicker, my country roots were appeased by our move to a more bucolic setting. The excitement of Boston was still there for it was only minutes away. The incredible high I got every time I saw the Boston skyline was satisfied by a quick trip down Commonwealth Avenue which dissected the city ending at the famous Boston Common. Our new neighborhood was surrounded by Newton Center and Chestnut Hill, two opulent areas distinctive by their English Tudor style homes. Recreation was an integral function of the area manifested by the many parks, playgrounds and jogging paths that enveloped the community. It was September, perhaps the most spectacular time in the northeast, and it seemed like the entire population of our new location was jogging, playing ball, or just enjoying the outdoors. Our old neighborhood had been characterized by an eclectic blend of the bazaar, the unusual, and the dangerous. To our delight, Chandler Pond offered a much more serene setting and a more appealing variety of mostly young, goal driven professionals mixed with ambitious, intellectual students. There seemed to be a sharing of a simple philosophy— work hard and play even harder. It was a philosophy that Baxter and I had no trouble adopting, as our apartment soon became the hub of our new complex. It only made sense that we utilize our centricity to host a welcome to Chandler Pond party for all the new tenants.

In Boston, parties were a happening. There was no reason to go to a great deal of trouble in planning the party. There were no formal invitations that needed to be sent because word just spread rapidly among the buildings. Bringing your own beverage was understood and hors d'oeuvres were optional. In our case, the option was never exercised. Maureen and Dale helped us plan the event and acted as hostesses. Needless to say, many of our new male neighbors were speechless when they came to the door and were greeted by these two gorgeous girls. We relished the fact that our first impression on our neighbors was enhanced by our association with Maureen and Dale. They had quickly become good friends and Baxter and I talked between ourselves about dating them at some time in the near future; but alas, Maureen was engaged to some mystery man a great deal older than she who we surmised was paying the rent. Dale was dating the Boston Bruins superstar, Bobby Orr, the most popular athlete in Boston whom every girl in the city had a crush on. Our fantasies aside, the girls shared many great moments with us. They were always quick to supply us with the female perspective on things and thankfully kept our growing male egos in check. For me they were taking the place of my sisters who I was seeing less and less frequently. The distance from home to Boston hadn't changed but the gap was continuing to grow.

Our small apartment quickly filled that night with the beautiful people of Boston, most of whom seemed to live in our complex. It was truly a great way for everyone to get to know their new neighbors. It was also a great way for Baxter and me to establish ourselves. This would be the first of many parties that we hosted and consequently our popularity among our peers was instantaneous. We enjoyed our new status and milked it for all it was worth. Baxter and I had been best friends for a long time and we were good together. He was the ladies man and I was the shy one. He was small, always tanned, and, in his words, "irresistible to girls." I was 6 inches taller, light skinned, and looked like Opie on the Andy Griffith Show. He was adventuresome and unafraid of experimenting in the many temptations of the time. I was conservative and positively afraid of getting into trouble. I was responsible; he wasn't. I was always picking up the apartment; he was always making a mess. He was the Yin and I was the Yang; yet somehow it worked. We respected each other's space, and rarely had a harsh word between us.

Our initial party, which lasted most of the night, was our new beginning. Life was good. The social opportunities were exploding. My job status continued to improve with the promotion at work and Baxter's new job seemed to be going well personally and financially. We were settling into a comfortable place. I believed for the first time since we left home that our move was going to work out and that I was where I was supposed to be. I finally felt like I belonged.

# Chapter Fifteen

## BACK TO THE IVIED WALLS

A S THE END of summer neared, my father completed his radiation treatments. His mood was noticeably more ebullient. He was back to his old self, more humorous and more attentive to those around him. The cancer was in remission and the prognosis was good. Cancer seemed like a shadow that followed his family. Both his parents and then his sister were victims. For the time being, at least, he felt like he had beaten the disease. For the first time in many years, he felt good and he was determined to stay that way. There would be no more drinking and, certainly, there would be no more smoking. His life had passed through many phases. He hoped that this new phase was going to be a positive one.

It was a summer I would never forget. Pat and Gary finally tied the knot after many years of dating. The wedding was a lavish one fueled by the resources of two well-to-do families. Like just about everything else in our lives, I shared Pat's happiness. Gary was a solid guy and a hard worker. Together they made a good team and it seemed they had the brightest of futures. They made it very clear to me that I was welcomed anytime at their house and Gary added menacingly that he expected me to visit often. It was funny how he could make an invitation sound like a threat, but that was just part of his charm. I told them that I would stay away until Pat was pregnant and that I wanted to be the Godfather. It wouldn't take long before my request was granted. For one day, the father-daughter conflict between two stubborn and proud people was set aside and my father beamed with pride for his youngest girl. He celebrated the wedding sober, a triumph we all shared with him.

For me, I not only established a relationship with my father that summer that had been missing most of my life, but also, I enjoyed the time I spent with mom in the dealership office. Up to that point, I had no idea how smart and capable my mother was. Stay-at-home moms were the rule in those days rather than the exception. I knew she could cook, and I knew she was a great mother of five kids. What I didn't know was that she was once an executive secretary in a large insurance company in Hartford. She had superb accounting and bookkeeping skills, was adept at balancing the day's receipts and was generally extremely efficient in running the dealership in my father's absence. She did a magnificent job that summer. She kept the business afloat and managed the personnel, including me, with the dexterity of an experienced boss. I was impressed! I wondered why I had never really known that much about my parents. It made me wonder just how self centered I really was.

With the good news about my father, it made the return to college for my senior year a great deal easier. I was anxious to see all my fraternity brothers and I couldn't wait to see Alix. She lived in New Jersey about three hours away. With my baseball schedule, our relationship had been reduced to long distance phone calls, and long, suggestive letters. A song came out that summer called, "See You in September" by the 'Happenings' and that had become our song. She was very understanding about my need to be home with my father, but unclear as to her understanding about my love of baseball. It was a mistress she was unprepared to accept. As much as I had enjoyed the summer, it was time to get back to school.

The Vietnam War hovered like a dark cloud over the goals and aspirations of college seniors. The draft awaited the 1968 graduating class putting any career plans on hold. An escalation in the war sparked by the "Tet offensive" on January 31st had soured the American people against the incumbent president, Lyndon Johnson. This led to his famous speech announcing his intentions not to run for another term as president.

Student riots protesting the war were becoming nightly clips on the national news. It was an intense time.

At Merrimack, the war was a constant topic of conversation, but riots were not yet a part of our culture. We were isolated in our innocence. Students acknowledged the war and its impact on our future, but we also obsessed about the hockey team and the basketball team, about student week, about exams, and about our relationships. We were in collective denial protected by the ivied walls of our suburban Catholic school. We would soon enough be affected by the horrible world around us, but for now we would enjoy a brief and happy respite.

# Chapter Sixteen

## START SPREADING THE NEWS

AT OUR INTRODUCTORY party, we met two young men and their wives who had moved into two adjacent apartments on our floor. There was an instant bantering that developed between us when we found out they were both from New York and brought with them all the baggage of being New York sports fans. For years in Connecticut we put up with the many New York faithful who split the fandom of the state. Connecticut was like Switzerland. It is geographically located between warring states and thus it harbored a division of fan loyalty. Until the improbable run of the 1967 Red Sox, we had little ammunition with which to argue with obnoxious Yankee fans. But the Celtics were a different story. For years, Celtic fans had the absolute upper hand. That upper hand, however, had taken a wrong turn in the early 70's as the Knicks became a power and the Celtics suffered through a couple years of mediocrity. The timing was horrible.

Bill and Larry were the antithesis of Baxter and me. Bill was born in New York City, attended Columbia and was now attending Boston College Law School. Like us, he was a former athlete who would rather compete in a game than watch one. Larry was also a New Yorker, but much more obnoxious. He graduated, as he always reminded us, from Cornell. He was employed at some big accounting firm in Boston and regularly left for work early in the morning in a three piece suit carrying a briefcase. He was a big guy, about 6 ft. 2 in., with a barrel chest that he pumped out every time the New York Knicks beat our beloved Celtics.

They were both married to lovely girls who were quite content to stay out of our constant arguments about sports, and who were understanding enough to allow their husbands to hang around with us. Celtic and Knicks games became events in our apartment and were usually followed by a two-on-two bloodbath at the student activity center at Boston College. The Knicks won most of the games that year but Baxter and I managed to exact our fair share of revenge on the courts at B.C. Our New York - Boston rivalry spilled over to the Bruins - Rangers and, of course, the Yankees - Red Sox. We argued a lot; we drank a great deal; and we played hard in our four man war of city supremacy. Through it all, almost predictably, we became good friends. Bill and Larry were an integral part of our life in Boston. We were never going to convince them that Boston was the better city, but one thing was for sure, we were having fun trying.

It had been months since Baxter heard from Anna. He knew she had gone back to Italy to see her family and ostensibly to stay away from him. He occasionally mentioned her but was busy filling in the lonely hours with a seemingly endless number of attractive dates that more often than not would stay the night and never come back. It was silly of me to try to be nice to any of them for I would never see them again. Bill, on the other hand, would always find a reason to visit when he saw Baxter coming home with yet another girl. He would hang around the apartment, drink a few beers and shake his head in disbelief. Bill had married very young and it was becoming apparent that he was envious of Baxter's lifestyle.

Bill's envy became frustration one day when he said to me: "What's he hung like a horse or something."

"No! I've showered with him after basketball games and he's no Milton Berle. He's more like Mickey Rooney."

"Then what's the attraction? How's he getting all these girls?"

"Bill, all he has to do is say he knows you and the girls can't wait to get here."

"Yeah that and a nickel might get him a cup of coffee."

"I'm afraid it's not nickels that's working for him. It's the pills!"

"Pills? What pills?"

"I don't really know," I said. "He gets them at his new job at the strip club."

"He's working at a strip club! When did this happen?"

"He left the German bar last week because it reminded him too much of Anna. He's been working at the Two O'clock Lounge on Washington Street in the Combat Zone. Most of his dates are girls he works with."

"The Combat Zone! Strippers! Pills! You guys are going to get me divorced just for thinking about all this."

Bill didn't know much about The Combat Zone. Law students didn't have much time to be traveling across town to forbidden areas. I explained to him that the Zone was an attempt by the city of Boston to centralize the sleazy bars and strip clubs and the unsavory characters that frequented these establishments in a two block area adjacent to China Town. It was a dangerous place, but like all such places the danger was the attraction.

Bill left our apartment that night again shaking his head. He would return the next day with more questions, but it was evident that he was becoming less satisfied with his own little cloistered world and was anxious to find out more about what Baxter was up to. He was ready for combat!

# *Chapter Seventeen*

## "SEE YOU WHEN THE SUMMERS THROUGH"

SINCE OUR LAST phone call, the anticipation of seeing Alix had built to a crescendo. As I waited somewhat impatiently for her parent's car to pull up to the girl's dorm, I replayed in my mind the moments that had led to the start of our relationship. When I first met her she was a year behind me in school, a freshman majoring in business administration. For some unknown reason, she surrounded herself with some very nice but unglamorous friends which insulated her from being noticed. Because I majored in English and consequently attended classes in a different part of campus, our paths never crossed. At meals in the student union, I always sat off to the side with my fraternity brothers and she sat inconspicuously with her friends. It was only by chance that I happened to stop at the concession area on the upper floor of the union. It was the first time I had ever been there and I was just going to stay long enough to pick up a term paper a girl pal had typed for me. As I sat at one of the four tables that dotted the small room, I noticed a demure petite girl with granny glasses sipping a coffee and concentrating intently on her text book. She was seated alone and obviously preferred it that way. There was something about her that distracted me; possibly it was her raven hair, or her big brown eyes, or the way her upper lip uncurled with her bewitching smile. I stole a long look and realized that under the disguise of a bookworm, there seemed to be a very pretty, very natural girl. When she stood up to refill her cup, I was stunned. Who was this girl and how come I had never seen her before?

As she returned to her table, I thought she gave me a slight nod which only made my blood pressure rise. Should I speak to her? I wasn't very good at that. I knew that my face had probably turned red, a cruel beacon alerting her of my intentions. I was about to leave when she said: "Hi! I'm Alix. Aren't you running for president of the junior class? I saw your speech. I thought you did a good job. Congratulations!"

I couldn't believe that she knew who I was. Thank God for politics. I fumbled with a pathetic response, which she said was endearing. Our conversation continued until it was time for her curfew. She asked if I wanted to walk her back to the girl's dorm, which I was able to do without falling on my face both literally and figuratively.

Our initial date the following weekend was to my first fraternity party as a new brother. Eight weeks of intensive pledging had left me exhausted and ready to reap the benefits of brotherhood. The party was in a rented hall in Lawrence, Mass., a few miles off campus. There was a live band and kegs of cold beer. My new brothers made a big deal of Alix making her feel welcome and comfortable. It was also her first frat party—obvious by the death grip she had on my left arm. We danced almost every song and awkwardly enjoyed our first slow dance together. I told her she fit perfectly in my arms and she responded that she felt very comfortable there. Her smile was just melting me although I tried in vain not to show my emotions. I was hooked for sure and it appeared she was as well. The party ended at midnight. As we left the hall, we were soaked by a torrential downpour. Laughing and hugging, we splashed our way to the car. Despite the rain, there was no way I wanted this evening to end, but Alix had a curfew so we headed back to campus. The car radio was playing contemporary music, much mellower than the raucous noise we had listened to all night. Alix sat next to me and laid her head on my shoulder. I was floating on a love cloud, falling in love with this beautiful, sweet girl who I had randomly met only a couple of days before. As we drove down a dark road in the rain, Frank

Sinatra began to sing the perfect song on the radio to end a perfect evening. We crossed under a bridge that spanned the road, and sheltered us from the blinding rain. I stopped the car and asked Alix if she wanted one last dance. She looked at me with eyes I would never get enough of and said she would love to. So there we were; two people who had just met, dancing to "Strangers in the Night" alone under a bridge, on a deserted road.

*Strangers in the night exchanging glances*

*Wondering in the night*

*What were the chances we'd be sharing love*

*Before the night was through.*


*Something in your eyes was so inviting,*

*Something in your smile was so exciting,*

*Something in my heart,*

*Told me I must have you.*


*Strangers in the night, two lonely people*

*We were strangers in the night.*

*Up to the moment*

*When we said our first hello.*

*Little did we know*

*Love was just a glance away,*

*A warm embracing dance away and —*

*Ever since that night we've been together.*

*Lovers at first sight, in love forever.*

*It turned out so right,*

*For strangers in the night.*

From those first awkward moments of our chance meeting, the beautiful days that accompanied the first weeks or even months of our new relationship followed and we became inseparable. It had, indeed, "turned out so right, for strangers in the night."

My daydreaming ended when I saw her parent's car turn into the road leading to the girl's dorm. After the appropriate greetings to her parents, I hugged the girl I hadn't seen in three months but thought about every day. She was radiant and more beautiful than I remembered. Everything was looking up until she asked where my baseball glove was. There appeared to be a great deal of sarcasm accompanying the remark and the dagger attached to the sarcasm seemed to be opening a fresh wound. I wondered where this was heading. When her parents said their goodbyes, I had my answer. They were barely out of sight when her obvious frustration unmasked itself. She kissed me and then started to cry. "I'm sorry," she said. "I told myself I wouldn't cry, but I missed you. It just seemed that your baseball buddies were more important to you than I was." I tried to console her as best I could, but she was right. I should have made an effort to go to New Jersey to see her during the summer, but she was also right that my baseball buddies were important to me. She had never been an athlete and didn't know how an athlete ticks so it was fruitless to mention playoffs or big games. It was equally fruitless to try to explain commitment to a team. Her only concern was the level of commitment that I had given her over the summer. We had been a couple for almost two years. Unfortunately, the bloom was off the rose.

# *Chapter Eighteen*

## WHILE THE WORLD BURNS

WHILE OUR LIVES in Brighton were filled with highlights of wild parties, new friends, and exciting forays into the decadence of the early 70's, the political landscape in Washington and around the world was crumbling with our country's futile involvement in a war that we were not going to win. President Nixon knew his legacy would be attached to his efforts to end this conflict that threatened to totally divide the nation. He also knew that his chance of being re-elected in the upcoming 1972 election was directly tied to his success in not only bringing home our troops from a war that most Americans thought was morally wrong, but also in the outcome of winning or losing the war. The United States had never been on the losing side of war.

During the latter part of 1970, American troop levels had dropped significantly, a clear concession to the growing dissent at home. It was made public that of the 280,000 troops still in Vietnam by year's end, over 60,000 had significant experimentation with drugs. It was also disclosed that many of the active units were plagued with racial unrest, again reflecting the disharmony back in the states.

On January 4, 1971, President Nixon announced "the end is in sight." He was, of course, historically wrong. Instead of de-escalation, U.S. fighter bombers launched a fierce bombardment of North Vietnamese Army supply camps in Laos and Cambodia.

The bombings sparked huge riots at home culminating in the mass arrest of over 12,000 protesters in Washington. In April, it was announced that the American death total had reached 45,000. Nixon's approval rating as a result of his new Vietnam strategy had slipped below 34 per cent. Facing an election in 1972, it was obvious that Nixon would have to turn the tide of the war in our favor and do it quickly. (Source information from: Vietnam War.com:TheVietnam War)

Although Baxter and I were in separate National Guard units, we were both on constant alert of being activated to either fight in Vietnam or to confront protesters here at home, most of whom were our age. There was a constant uneasiness that pervaded our everyday existence. When we heard of the escalation in Vietnam and the resultant student and racial unrest, we decided to handle the situation in the best way we knew how—we would have a party!

We spread the word through our tenant network that this was going to be the party to beat all others. It wasn't a celebration like many of our other get-togethers, but rather this party was going to be an event to ease the tensions of the times. This was going to be like Fat Tuesday in New Orleans before Ash Wednesday.

Partiers came from everywhere. There were many people from my work, including: executive secretaries; young, single scientists without a thimble of social skills; and members of my contract group from the home office in Quincy, Mass. There were also people from all over the neighborhood, and even people who had heard about the party in different sections of Boston. It was the most diverse crowd of merrymakers we ever had. As the crowd continued to grow, the party spilled out into the hallway and eventually outside onto the landscaped lawn between our three apartment buildings. Couples were seen making out on the lawn and behind the bushes and on blankets down by the pond. What started out as a party to forget the scary times we were living in was becoming a love fest. Nobody had an agenda to disrupt the party and consequently partiers were simply just getting along and having a good time. There were young professionals sharing joints with longhaired freaky people. There were students conversing metaphysically with strippers from Baxter's bar. Two professional hockey players from the Bruins were showing some computer nerds from MIT how to shoot a slap shot. Stewardesses from four different airlines that lived in the complex became the targets of the young professional set, lawyers and accountants and brokers. Diversity seemed to be the theme of the night.

Bill and Larry came without their wives. Both were astonished by the happenings around them. Bill had developed a fascination with strippers since he learned of Baxter's new job and was concentrating too intently for a married man on the three girls from the Combat Zone. He had obviously smoked something funny before he came because all he would do was walk up to one of the girls and instead of speaking, he would just giggle. Larry watched from a quiet corner all that was going on and just smiled and drank his beer. After all, Larry was from Cornell and Ivy Leaguers had to maintain their dignity. A couple of dogs snuck in when the door was left open and moved furtively about under the glow of a black light, unnoticed while they snacked on whatever food was left unattended. There was plenty of beer, plenty of wine, and plenty of the cigarettes Bill liked to smoke. This wasn't a party for the meek and mild. The record player blared a host of psychedelic music, which soothed the pressure of the world from which we were trying to escape. Prominent were the words of Bob Dylan: "Everybody let's get stoned." Somehow over the din of noise, we heard the phone ring. It was Anna. She was back in town.

# Chapter Nineteen

## AN INTRODUCTION TO MARRIAGE

DURING THE SEMESTER break my senior year, I came back to Connecticut for what would be the last time before graduation. I needed to come home to address a new development in my relationship with Alix. I sought the advice of the two people in the world I knew would not only provide a sympathetic ear, but would also supply me with a possible solution. I had to see my sister June and her husband, Rick. On those rare occasions when I would come home during my four years in college, I would often visit my sister. Her house was like a refuge for the confused and the distraught. She had a wondrous sense of logic and compassion and an innate ability to advise without preaching.

Rick was the perfect compliment to June. He understood women and relationships better than anyone I knew, and he readily poured out his advice along with his ever present bourbon on the rocks. The combination of these two caring people, who were the parents of three very active young sons, was just the medicine I needed. I also knew the bourbon would help.

My problems were twofold. I knew that by the end of the year, with military service waiting ahead, I would have to make a decision on my permanent plans with Alix. Added to my indecision was her recent declaration that she was afraid of having kids. She said kids terrified her and she felt that her life would be full enough without them. I wondered if she was just getting sick of me and was using this latest statement to discourage me from making any long-range commitment. I needed a second opinion.

It was not unusual for me to seek the consult of June and Rick. It was unusual that I went to see them alone. Whenever I told my friends I was going over to their house, they wanted to come. The general opinion of my buddies was that a visit to my sister's house was a glimpse ahead into the ideal world of a perfect marriage. They all liked Rick for his gregarious personality, his generosity with his liquor, and his readiness to engage in political, social, or philosophical debates on a myriad of topics. Rick was the consummate host, greeting all visitors with a warm smile and a strong handshake. The real attraction, however, was my sister. All my friends, without exception, simply loved June. Baxter, the flirtatious rogue of our group, had a huge crush on her. He thought she was a goddess, too good to be true. Charlie and Mike, both University of Connecticut seniors, thought Rick and June were perfect together and hoped their relationship would someday be a blueprint to follow in their own lives. Mike, a philosophy major, and Charlie, an engineering student, looked forward to the discussions with Rick in the living room. The discussions were always lively and interesting.

Baxter was a graduate of a culinary institute and was working as a bartender. He was quite content to hang around the kitchen with June while the rest of us were debating the issues of the day. We would kid him after we left that he spent so much time in the kitchen that some day he would make somebody a good wife. I'm sure June was flattered by all the attention Baxter showed her, but she never let on that she was wise to him. It was part of her charm that she could deflect the romantically hopeless without crushing their dream. It didn't matter to her whether you were the best looking or the most popular or whether you had warts on your nose. She accepted you as you were and, in Baxter's case, she accepted him for the incorrigible flirt that he was.

There was a 10-year age difference between June and me. There had always been a bond of the big sister looking after her youngest brother. She was the one who supported me whenever I felt like the world was coming down on me. It was time to ask for that support once again. This time, I went to their house alone.

Rick had always preached to me that a lasting relationship had to be with the right girl, at the right time, in the right place. Without all three, the relationship wouldn't work. He then added that I should look at a girl and picture her as the mother of my kids. If the picture didn't come across clearly, then that girl was not the one. There was no doubt in my mind that Alix was the right girl. She consumed my heart. We were in a good place, at least temporarily, but was it the right time? As far as kids were concerned, I could picture her as a mother, but was her reluctance to have kids a permanent fear? Rick knew I wanted kids and he said he knew I would be a good father by the way I handled and played with his three boys. He told me I was born to be a father. "Someday you'll be a coach and you'll enjoy every minute of it," he said. June added that maybe Alix stated she was afraid to have children to get a reaction out of me—to find out whether I was serious about a long term commitment. She said, "if you truly love her then you're going to have to confront her on the parenting issue and then be prepared to commit to marriage in the future. She's a beautiful girl, Sean. She won't wait for you forever." I left their house knowing that I was about to face the biggest decision of my life. I prayed that night for the inspiration to make the right choice.

# Chapter Twenty

## THE DATING GAME

IT WAS NOT unusual for me to work late. Overtime was the only way I could supplement my frozen income. It was, however, unusual that Baxter would call me at work when I was at the office after hours. The call came around eight o'clock. Baxter was in a panic.

"Sorry to bother you, but I need your help. Can you get home early?"

"I guess so. What's the problem? Some pimp after you?"

"Worse than that. I've got Jenny here at the apartment."

"And...?"

"And Anna just called again. She's back in Boston and she's on her way over. She said she wanted to surprise me. I couldn't tell her about Jenny. She would flip out again and God knows what she'd do. Can you hurry and take Jenny home. She lives in Waltham."

"I'm on my way", I said, not knowing what was in store for me when I got there.

Jenny was the first girl Baxter had dated in months that was a decent and sweet person. She was cute and sharp and obviously had fallen for Baxter's lines. He had seen her a couple of times and appeared to be a good match for him. It was like Anna somehow sensed the danger of a new girl in Baxter's life. She was about to make her grand return.

I arrived at the apartment literally moments before Anna's cab. I whisked Jenny out the side door and off we went slithering into the night. The ride home was uncomfortable as I was getting grilled about what just happened. Jenny was sniffling, then openly crying. I was disgusted with Baxter for putting me in this situation. My mission was accomplished as I got Jenny home safely although spiritually damaged. I tried my best to console her and in the process we struck up a nice rapport. She even hinted, as we sat in front of her house, that maybe she picked the wrong roommate; but there was no way I was going to go there. Baxter and I never messed in the other's business. We had established an unspoken roommate's code that provided sovereignty over our own stables of girls. Violation of the code would have led to all-out war. I said goodnight and searched for the nearest bar to have a drink. As I settled into a nearly empty corner pub somewhere in Waltham, I began to ruminate about my life in Boston and the relationships that I seemed to be very good at screwing up. I came to the conclusion that my problem was that I pursued the unavailable and avoided the eligible. It wasn't for any lack of opportunity for there were many. I ordered another bourbon. There was something soothing about the taste of bourbon. Whatever the perceived medicinal benefits, there was definitely a calm that came over me whenever I put a Jack Daniels in my hand. It cleared the cobwebs from my cluttered mind and allowed me to drift into a dream-like trance where I could recount the more memorable Boston experiences.

For two years I lived in fantasy land. The floors of NASA proved a fertile playground for an erstwhile dating history. Subsequently I dated a liberal cross section of nationalities, religions, race, size and looks. As the experience of trying to be original and entertaining on too many different occasions turned burdensome, I became more and more selective. The slightest identifiable flaw I detected in these girls would end any chance of a more permanent relationship. I often kidded Baxter as I was leaving for a date that if I was home for the 11 o'clock news, my ever-vigilant radar had detected some imperfection, no matter how inconsequential, and therefore I was headed home for the evening newscast. It was a pursuit of the perfect girl made more difficult by the continued comparisons with Alix. I was beginning to wonder who the hell I thought I was. I was judging a whole lot of very nice girls against standards that in no way would I stand up to if the situation reversed itself. I wasn't trying to hurt anyone and I wasn't mean or unflattering to anybody—I was just emotionally unavailable. It's funny how human nature works for the more distant and cool I acted with these girls, the more they became interested.

Oh, there had been moments when things could have worked out with some very attractive and appealing women. For example, I had a brief fling with Roberta, the executive secretary to the branch manager at NASA. She was a knockout, very classy and very sexy. Even though we got along famously and had a great time together, she didn't consider my position in life to be up to her standards. She was in love with her married boss, which made her safe for me to see, but unavailable for a serious relationship.

Then there was Marsha, the most extraordinary of all the girls I met during this time. She was a beautiful Jewish girl who lived in our apartment complex and also worked at NASA. We would drive together to work every day. She made it very easy to fall for her because she was just so lovely in every sense. But road blocks were a big part of my life and Marsha, despite our mutual attraction, explained that she was pledged to marry a man who was twenty years older than she. He was a lawyer and most important to her family, he was Jewish. She explained that there was no way she could ever be with anyone who wasn't Jewish. Her parents just simply wouldn't approve. It was my first rejection for religious reasons.

I ordered another bourbon and dug deeper into a memory bank of dates that were scarred by failure of one kind or another. It was like referring to a Rolodex list of the doomed. They came and went, some more memorable than others. There were the two Chinese secretaries from the typing pool, attractive and delicate creatures. The first was cute but was a definite cultural mismatch.

She lasted one full date and one early newscast. The other was way too promiscuous for a serious relationship, although we kept her around for our parties. Next there was Geraldine, a self described witch who must have lived in Salem at one time and whose Gothic look scared me to death, and also scared me away. She became angry with me at one of our parties for kissing another guest behind the bar. She left in anger threatening to cast a spell on me for embarrassing her. Based on some of the things that happened to me over the next few years, I think she was successful.

After that debacle, I wandered downtown to Park Square to check out the action at some of the sleazy joints where there was no chance of finding anyone normal. I discovered a small bar next to the Playboy Club that had one of the last Burlesque shows in Boston. It was kind of a hidden gem of a bar where they mixed stripping with actual singing. The main performer was a thirty-something torch singer named Judy Whitney, whose raspy singing voice and extraordinary body immediately got my attention. Because of Judy I became a regular and over the next couple of weeks, we became good friends. She was a former Vegas performer whose red hair and personality spun a web of intrigue over my innocent, infatuated heart until one day she introduced me to her mafia boyfriend. Our fling ended quickly. Mama didn't raise a fool.

At Baxter's bar, I continued my voyage into the sordid life. I met one of the dancers, Peggy Please, a leggy, black performer who invited me to visit her at her apartment on a Saturday afternoon. I had never dated a black girl and I was excited thinking about what was obviously going to be a memorable experience. I had to break the date because of work and she never spoke to me again.

The best of all, however, was the statuesque blonde go-go dancer I met at another sordid joint in Park Square. She had once danced on the 60's TV hit, "Hullabaloo". She was strikingly beautiful and seemed to like me a great deal but when she wore high heels, she was about 8 inches taller. There is such a thing as too much woman and she certainly was.

Dating girls from the apartment provided a whole different challenge. Despite my philosophy that you don't dump where you eat, I found some of the girls in the building too cute to resist. Phyllis, a dental hygienist, really knew how to clean your teeth. She lived just down the hall, never far enough away to visit at strange hours. Phyllis became a lifelong friend and friends don't date. Upstairs in our building lived Amy and Mimi who were roommates attending Boston University. They both loved to party and were regular fixtures at our monthly gatherings. All three were very attractive as were many others in the building. Mimi, however, was the one that I liked the most; but that Jewish thing came up again and stood like a blockade against establishing any kind of relationship. I was beginning to consider converting to Judaism or at least getting circumcised.

There were simply too many choices for someone as confused as me. The ones I liked were taken either by antiquated religious beliefs; by older, more established men; by a fear of my white, Irish-Catholic heritage; by lesbianism; or by any other myriad, hard-to-fathom reason which could kill a relationship before it started. The ones I had no interest in would swarm like mosquitoes sensing an opportunity to suck the blood out of a living, breathing, potential boyfriend. It was very much like navigating through a maze of opportunities never knowing if the results were going to be rewarding or hazardous to my health. Ever fearful, I navigated on.

# Chapter Twenty-One

## FOR GOD AND COUNTRY

RETURNING TO SCHOOL for my last semester was distressing. My thought processes were in shambles; my rational thinking was unraveled; and my concentration, once indefatigable, was shaken. I was quickly distracted and easily angered. I knew from the reactions of those around me whom I cared about, that there was concern for where my head was at and worry that my volatile Irish temper would eventually get me into some kind of trouble. I worried too, for my mind was sinking into a deep hole of indecision where I was incapable of discerning the absurd from the normal. Faced with an uncertain future due to military commitment, I feared that I would make the wrong choices concerning my relationship with Alix. I wondered if I would be better off without her, and I eventually convinced myself that she would be better off without me. I thought I got my answer one afternoon in early spring when I went for a ride in the country surrounding the campus. I turned on the radio to an oldies station and the first song to play was like listening to the harbingers of fate. It was a song by the Lovin' Spoonful' and its words struck home.

> "Did you ever have to make up your mind
> Pick up on one and leave the other behind
> It's not often easy and not often kind
> Did you ever have to make up your mind."

I went quickly back to the dorm and confided in my two best friends in the fraternity, John and Joe that I was thinking of breaking up with Alix. The four of us often hung around together and referred to ourselves as the 'four musketeers'. They both liked Alix a great deal and often told me that she was way too good for me. You know, you hear something enough times and you begin to believe it. I also believed my depressed mood was a reaction to our time together in college running out. I thought long and hard about how next year at this time I would be in some rice patty in Vietnam while Alix would be enjoying her senior year at Merrimack. I envisioned the very nice but merciless Dear John letter I would receive informing me that she met someone else. My imagination was playing tricks on me and leading to many sleepless nights. This all led  to my declaration to John and Joe that I needed a change.

I was surprised by their reaction as I expected both of them to defend Alix and try to talk me out of it. Instead they thought that based on my recent behavior and my obvious angst over my future, it was the smart thing to do. Joe, who was the star point guard on the basketball team, used a basketball analogy by saying: "If the game plan's not working, change it." He added that he had no idea how difficult it was for me because he still had another year to go. John, fondly nicknamed Jug, was the fraternity clown and made some reference to being foot loose and fancy-free until Uncle Sam gets you. He said, "We're both going to be in some god forsaken jungle next year being shot at by hundred pound Vietnamese soldiers who look like children; so what difference will it make? Give her a break and let her meet some other schmuck while we're on vacation in Southeast Asia. If you come back and still have two arms, two legs, and can still pee without a shot of penicillin, then maybe you can give her a call and see if she remembers you."

John then offered to set me up on a blind date and dared me to have the balls to be seen at a basketball game with this girl. It was a dare that I took and immediately regretted. The girl meant nothing to me but the outcome was all too predictable. What was I thinking? What possible reason did I have for doing this to my girlfriend? I was in an emotional freefall.

Alix was stunned that I would do such a thing and hurt that I would do it in public where her friends were quick to inform her of my infidelity. I wanted to crawl under a big rock. It was just another in a long line of poor decisions I was making and unfortunately for me, this one cost me the girl that I loved. After a few feeble attempts on my part to patch up our shattered affair, I found myself sitting in my car by myself at my graduation pondering my suddenly hopeless future. Instead of looking ahead in a positive way, I was looking back with remorse and a great deal of self pity. A week after I received my diploma, I received a letter from my local draft board scheduling me for a physical to prepare for entry into the U.S. Army.

It was a tough time to be a draftee. The war in Vietnam was raging since the "Tet" offensive that had turned the tide of the war in the favor of the North Vietnamese. College graduates were no longer able to file for all kinds of deferments and the lottery didn't go into effect until 1969. It didn't matter who you knew or didn't know because when your time came to be drafted, you were expected to serve. Many eligible candidates for the draft fled to Canada and denounced their American citizenship. It was a contentious time where students rallied against the war and protested their eligibility for the draft by burning their draft cards. It was a nightly news occurrence to see students in some part of the country banning together to protest an unpopular war. Some of these protests turned violent and unrest ruled the evening airways. It felt like the world was about to explode. Soldiers were chastised for the uniform they wore and ridiculed by the vocal minority of young people who were against anyone or anything that represented the war. It was an unlikely conflict of two factions of young Americans, one following the traditional path of serving God and country and the other following the path of protest of traditional values. Our Constitution gave the right to every American to protest and express an opinion, but the line was crossed when the very liberties they were protesting were endangered by the violence of their actions. I was about to take the side of the traditional although I was unsure as to which side I was actually on.

# Chapter Twenty-Two

## A CUP OF COFFEE IN THE SUN

"I GUESS THAT'S it. I guess it's finally over. It was like she sensed someone was here. I kept denying it and played dumb, but she just kept accusing me of cheating on her even before she left for Italy. If she could have, she would have broken every dish and lamp in the apartment. I'm lucky she didn't physically harm me. You're fortunate you weren't here because she blamed you too for being a bad influence on me. What a night!"

It wasn't the first time I had seen Baxter in a mess over a girl. He was ruthless and could have cared less if someone's feelings were hurt. He thought of girls like they were goal tenders on a hockey team and it was his job to try to score. I had to admit some of the goal tenders were pretty hot, yet Anna was different. She controlled the game for most of their relationship but when things started to change, when her dominance was in question, she became hostile and destructive. Baxter found out the hard way that there was, indeed, "no fury like a woman scorned."

"You know, Bax, it was no picnic for me either. I had a hysterical young sweetheart crying all over my new shirt. I've got mascara stains on both sleeves and on my collar. You owe me big time for this one."

"Oh, who cares anyway? I'm better off without both of them. I'm leaving for Connecticut Friday morning for my two week National Guard summer camp at Camp Drum in New York so you've got the apartment to yourself. Maybe you'll get lucky."

With that bit of encouragement, he laughed; but I knew that deep down in that callous soul, he would miss Anna. He would never admit it and he rarely ever mentioned her name again, but you just don't forget someone like Anna. She was truly unique. I could honestly say I wasn't sorry to see her go, but I too would miss her for she was part of our lives. Two years of memories aren't erased that quickly. An era, however good or bad, had ended.

With Baxter gone for a couple of weeks and all the drama seemingly gone as well, I looked forward to a peaceful few days. Because I had worked a lot of overtime earlier in the week, my boss said I could leave at noon on Friday. It was a brutally warm early June day. The cloudless sky provided no relief to the inhabitants of Chandler Pond who like an entire generation of baby boomers were relishing the pursuit of a perfect tan. When I arrived home to my apartment shortly after midday, the first thing I noticed was the large number of blankets and people that had descended onto the field adjacent to the pond. It was a startling but welcomed sight after the many months of a tough winter. I went inside and decided to get a cup of coffee before I went back to see if any of my buddies were around. I spotted Bill and Larry off in the distance. It appeared Bill was smoking his ever present joint and Larry was planted next to a cooler of beer. It wasn't unusual to smoke marijuana in public in those days. At times it seemed like the whole city was stoned. I never saw Larry smoke anything and really didn't put much significance to that observation. However, it was odd that he was away from his job in the middle of the day. They spotted me standing on the hill overlooking the scene below and waved me over. Still dressed in my shirt and tie from work, I shouted to them that I was going to change first.

The smell of tanning lotion was evident in the air, blending nicely with the smells of early spring. It was one of those moments when you just stopped and enjoyed the great New England transition from the winter doldrums to the promise of the great weather ahead. Old Charlie Dickens hit it right on the nose when he called such moments, " the best of times".

As I was finishing my coffee and was about to go back to the apartment, I heard a familiar female voice say: "Hi, Sean. What are you doing home all dressed up in this heat?" Nancy, a girl who lived in one of the other buildings stood up from her blanket which was only a few feet away and waved me over. I had only met Nancy once before at one of our parties but remembered her as being a bit aloof. I actually thought she was kind of a bitch, but she seemed pleasant enough on this hot day. As I went over to her blanket, I notice there was another girl with her. "This is Katie, Sean. She and I work together as nurses at Saint Elizabeth's Hospital." Katie was very cute and quite bubbly. She had a beautiful, easy smile, golden brown hair that went half way down her back, and huge blue eyes that matched the brilliance of the June sky. As I was checking her out and trying not to be obvious, one of Bill's favorite sayings crossed my mind, "There were no flies on this girl."

"Why are you drinking hot coffee on such a warm day?" Katie asked seemingly more interested in my answer than the question warranted. I couldn't help myself as I answered, "that it was scientifically proven that drinking something warm on a hot day actually cools off your extremities." There was absolutely no proof to this absurd remark but it did elicit an endearingly naive response of, "Really! I guess that makes sense when you think about it." I thought to myself that she was adorable but seemed very gullible. They invited me to sit down for a few minutes and I readily accepted. Nancy was trying to dominate the conversation, but I was only interested in finding out more about Katie. I asked her where she was from. She said, "Beverly, Mass." I responded by saying that my high school principal had moved to Beverly after I graduated. I knew she was a few years younger so I wondered if she also had him as a principal. She did indeed. Bingo!

She then asked me where I went to college. When I told her Merrimack, she said her brother went there. Bingo, number two! When it was discovered that her brother and I both graduated in 1968, triple Bingo. Who said coincidence doesn't have a role in our lives. As the heat and the sun started to bake my sensitive Irish skin, I pardoned myself and said that I hoped that I would see her again. She said that would be nice, a clear opening that I didn't catch onto until after I left. I hoped that I would run into Katie again—much sooner than later. Thankfully, my wishes were granted.

# Chapter Twenty-Three

## MY GUARDIAN ANGEL

WITH ALIX NOW only a memory, I retreated back home with my diploma in hand to face the uncertainty of military service. It wasn't that I objected to fighting for my country; it was the fact that I had just spent four years preparing for a future and now all I had to look forward to was a jungle address in some far off country ravished by years of war. With my heart broken and my spirits shattered, the invitation from the draft board to join them for a physical was the icing on the cake. Depression had overtaken my whole body. I was listless and prone to sleeping at strange hours of the day. This, I thought to myself, was no way to celebrate graduating from college.

At my lowest point, I got a call from Baxter who insisted I join him and the guys for a few drinks. I reluctantly agreed although I warned him I might not be very good company. We went to a local bar and seven of my closest friends sat at a round table and took turns buying pitchers of cheap beer. Baxter had just come back from basic training with the Army National Guard and now was looking at five and a half more years of service as a "weekend warrior". Pete had also completed his active duty obligation and his brother, Charlie, was scheduled to go to reserve training in a couple of weeks. Dennis, Bob, Mike and I were facing the real thing. The Guard announced that there were no more openings at that time leaving the rest of us with no option other than permanent active duty. We found courage in each other's fate that night—four college grads all looking for answers and finding only a future carrying a rifle, fighting an enemy we had nothing against, for a cause we couldn't identify.

The night progressed, the alcohol took over, and the stories that were told at that table became more and more entertaining. These were my lifelong friends and just sharing with them some magical moments of laughter and camaraderie was the elixir I needed to raise my spirits from the depths of despair. I loved these guys and even though the future would be unfair to some of us, my love for them would never change.

The following week, Mike and Bob enlisted in the army. Dennis flunked his physical and was granted a medical deferment. Bob was one of the first of our group to go to Vietnam where he served in an artillery company. Although his hearing was never the same, he came home safely a year later. Mike was part of a military police unit that was sent to Korea. He actually enjoyed his time in Korea and often wrote letters home describing the beautiful Korean girls he was meeting on his tour of duty. After his year was over, Mike also came home safely. Some of our other friends didn't fare as well. Two guys from our high school class were permanently maimed by the shrapnel from rounds of mortar fire. One lost an eye and the other the fingers on his left hand. Another buddy from our football team was so emotionally damaged by the horrors of war that he literally spent the remaining years of his life sitting in the dark in a closet of his parent's home. He died years later having never spoken to anyone but his parents the rest of his life. It was a nasty war with many ghastly stories. The worst part for these young men, who answered the call to serve their country, was coming home to face ridicule from their peers. They were outcasts in the new society of counter culture anarchists. The youth of America was clearly divided by this unpopular and, in many ways, this unjustified war.

For me, my guardian angels were working overtime. When Gary heard that there were no more openings in the local Guard unit, he made a call to his unit in the neighboring town. Gary had joined this same unit a year before and his timely call resulted in hearing of an opening that would be quickly filled if I didn't act right away. I immediately drove to the unit and signed up. Within a month I was on my way to basic training at Fort Leonard Wood, Missouri as the newest member of the Connecticut National Guard. Pat and I had seen too little of each other the last couple of years, but I was at least content in the knowledge that she was with a good guy, a guy who had just kept me out of Vietnam. Baxter drove me to the train that took me to the airport and on the way left me with this little encouragement. "When you get back from basic, you and I are going to blow this town. Maybe we'll move to Boston. That will give you something to dream about when you're building bridges and bivouacking in zero degrees on the Snake River."

# Chapter Twenty-Four

## A DATE TO REMEMBER

"HI! HOW YA doing? Where are we going tonight?" Katie was bubbling over as she took her seat in my Pinto.

"I thought I'd surprise you," I said as I settled in behind the steering wheel. "I thought I would take you someplace where I can introduce you to some of my relatives and where there is also an amusement ride."

"Really! Wow, now I'm all excited. Can't you tell me any more than that?"

"No, I don't want to spoil the surprise. We'll be there soon enough."

I could tell Katie had a great zest for life. In the wrong hands, she could be vulnerable to deceit for she was as gullible and trusting as any girl I've ever dated. Unless my first impression was wrong, I didn't have to worry about seeing any news at eleven this night. I thought she was cute as hell. It would just be a matter of whether or not she tolerated my deviousness. Her reaction to my surprise would be interesting to see. This one, I thought to myself, could be a winner. However, I've thought that before and have been often disappointed. At any rate, we were off to a good start.

It was a short drive to our destination, but Katie filled the minutes with a seemingly unstoppable rhetoric that was in answer to my simple question of what had she been up to lately. It didn't take me long to figure out that this girl had a true gift of conversation, one that somehow avoided being onerous while covering every possible aspect of a topic. It certainly took the pressure off me to provide interesting small talk because it didn't appear that she was going to run out of breath anytime soon. As potentially annoying as her babbling on and on could have been, her personality and engaging smile made it quite bearable. I think I was infatuated.

We arrived at our destination and her face just lit up with anticipation. We were in Copley Square and we were entering the fantastically opulent and grand Copley Square Hotel. Once we entered through the gilded doors, I directed her to the lounge adjacent to the lobby. "This is the Merry-Go-Round Bar," I told her. "We can sit on the carousel section surrounding the bar and enjoy a 360 degree view of the entire room. The food and drinks are delicious and it's just a great place to enjoy the music of the small orchestra off in the corner. I hope you like it here!"

"It's beautiful", she answered, suddenly at a loss for words.

I sensed the need for me to take over the conversation, so I told her to look around at all the large portraits of aristocracy from previous centuries that adorned the high walls of the bar. I pointed out a couple of red faced princely types and told her they were my great uncles—Thaddeus, the prince of Worcester, and Tobias, the duke of New Bedford. I told her they were relatives from my mother's side of the family who helped build this beautiful building. All she could say was, "Wow!" It was refreshing to take someone out who hadn't been everywhere and done everything. Katie was genuinely a very nice albeit a very naive girl. I would have to make a mental note not to take advantage of that in the future, but for tonight a little flight of the fanciful was a way to show her I had imagination and a sense of humor. The evening was progressing rather nicely when I realized she was getting bombed on her margarita. She only had a few sips of her drink when she became giddy and shifted toward me on her elbows. She said she wasn't very good at drinking, a fact I again filed in my memory under future considerations.

"Do you want to get off this carousel before you get dizzy?"
I said before she got dizzier.

"Sure," she slurred. "Where do you want to go now?"

I said let's walk around and see the sights. We left the lounge
and I showed her the layout of the rather extensive lobby. As we
wandered down a hallway that led to a large ballroom and banquet
facility, I pointed out another portrait on the wall identifying it
as another relative. She was incredulous. "Are you rich?" she said.
I laughed in response keeping the charade alive. It was June 17,
1972. The moon was out over a perfect Boston skyline. The city
was awakening to the sights and sounds of the much anticipated
summer months; I was on a date that I was thoroughly enjoying;
and suddenly, visible through the front doors of the hotel, was a
large fire in a building just across the square. We were told the
fire was engulfing the Hotel Vendome, an historic hotel on the
corner of Dartmouth Street and Commonwealth Avenue. Katie
and I decided to go out into Copley Square to get a better look.
A large throng of people had gathered making it difficult to see.
We walked across the square to the steps of the Boston Public
Library, which afforded us a clear view of the blazing fire. As
we stood on the steps of the Library, I put my arm around Katie
to support her. She looked into my eyes and we kissed. It was a
magical kiss that I hoped we would duplicate many times in the
future. Unknown to us at the time was the fact that the fire at
the Hotel Vendome was a horrible catastrophe that included the
loss of nine firefighters. Somehow, through the triumph of a great
first date and the tragedy of a deadly fire, our love had been born.
Later that night, we heard that in Washington,D.C. five men were
arrested attempting to break into and wiretap the Democratic
Party offices in the Watergate Hotel. The future ramifications of
this arrest would rock the already unstable Nixon administration
and eventually lead to its demise. Our first date had indeed been
a memorable one. Because of the other historical events of the
evening, June 17, 1972 would be an easy date to remember.

# Chapter Twenty-Five

## FOLLOWING THE YELLOW BRICK ROAD

BOOT CAMP WAS everything I had heard it would be. It was amazing how the army has figured out how to brainwash its recruits without them knowing it. It was also amazing how a day could be so long and yet a week could be so short. Before I knew it, basic training was over and advanced infantry training began. Baxter was right about bivouacking on the river in the middle of winter. It was unbearably cold but because we were a bridge building company, we had to train to build bridges in all kinds of weather. We finished our week on the river with a fifty-mile forced march through the woods. With the physical condition we were in after sixteen weeks of intensive training, the forced march was a piece of cake. We had become fighting machines capable of going anywhere to confront our enemies. These weren't the normal soldiers that were graduating to the core of combat ready warriors. Over seventy-five per cent of my platoon were college graduates. Again, it was a sign of the times that our Army was highly skilled and most were highly educated. Many strong friendships developed with the guys I trained with and the disturbing thing for me was that I was considered a two per center, a member of the National Guard. The other ninety-eight per cent were regular army. At the end of boot camp, the guardsmen were going home while the regulars were being sent around the world with most going directly to Vietnam. It was tough saying good-bye to guys you have just gone through hell with and with whom you've bonded through sixteen weeks of rigorous training in extreme conditions. These guys were the true fabric of what America stood for. These were America's best. A day never passed that I didn't pray for their safe journey back to their homes and an end to this foolish war.

Coming back home meant facing an uncertain future. My aspirations for success, once so tied to my relationship with Alix and the preparation for a career after college, were now placed on a back burner while I tried to figure out who I was and what I wanted to be. I had grown up quite a bit while at basic training, but it was difficult translating that maturity into a viable career path. I knew I wasn't alone. Jobs were scarce, especially in Northeastern Connecticut, which was an industrial area where most of the labor force were blue-collar workers. After four years in college and a stint in the service, I wasn't looking for a factory job.

"Why don't you ask your father for a job?" my mother offered knowing the difficult time I was having finding work. "He could use a good salesman. You know a lot of people in the area and I think you'd be excellent." Her opinion of me had never varied. She thought I was capable of accomplishing anything. She also knew, however, that I had stated on many occasions that I would never go into the car business. My father and I had breeched a lifelong impasse in our relationship during the chauffeured trips to Hartford Hospital two summers before, but I never felt comfortable in the thought that we could work together on a daily basis. His personality and sardonic way of looking at things were too close to my own. I imagined there would be clashes and most likely bitter arguments. I wanted to avoid ruining what we had taken so long to establish. My mother seemed quite disappointed with my answer for she knew that my only option to find the kind of work I was looking for was to leave the area and perhaps move to a city. I could tell she was frightened that her youngest child wouldn't be able to handle life outside our cozy little town. She was worried for my safety.

That afternoon, Baxter and I played some basketball on the playground behind the grammar school. He was also having a difficult time finding the right job, and his parents were bugging him to settle down. His only way of getting away with some of the things he did was to lie to his parents and say he was with me. His parents were very strict since Baxter's only brother had been killed in a car accident. They trusted me and were happy when Baxter and I hung around together. But Baxter liked to be devious and he would sneak around with various loose girls and stay out late at night drinking and carousing. His parents would tolerate it because he would always say he was with me. I was his best friend and his alibi.

Basketball was secondary on our minds that day as we discussed plans for the future. After several poor suggestions, we came up with Boston. Beantown! Home of the Red Sox --- the Celtics --- and the Bruins! We didn't figure out the logistics of the move until later, but we were excited about our choice. This wasn't going to be some silly idea to be stored away in our imagination. We were going to do this—and, the sooner, the better!

# *Chapter Twenty-Six*

## AN ASTRONAUT BY ANY OTHER NAME

"**A**RE YOU AN Astronaut?"

That was the question I knew Katie would eventually pose when I told her I worked at NASA. For a brief moment I thought about stringing her along with my best tales of Neil Armstrong and me, but the rewards reaped from such a tale would be less than satisfying because they would have been too easy. I liked this girl and I didn't want her to think I was making fun of her. She was no dummy. She was a very competent nurse who worked in the very busy emergency room at St. Elizabeth's. She dealt with life threatening situations on a daily basis. She was extremely bright and conversant on almost any subject. Most importantly, to me she was the best looking girl in the hospital and looked great in a nurse's uniform. She was just so gullible and naive that she needed somebody like me to guide her through the pitfalls that could imperil someone like her who believed everything you say.

"No," I said amazing even myself at my self-restraint, "I work as an editor on the publications floor. We edit and rewrite the scientific data supplied to us by NASA scientists. Without us, nothing would happen at NASA."

"Oh come on," she said, "you're really an Astronaut, aren't you?"

Katie and I had spent most of the week together following our big date. We were still getting to know one another and having a great time. Baxter was due back from his two weeks at

Camp Drum and I couldn't wait for him to meet Katie. I warned her that her naivete would be a weakness that Baxter would pick up on quickly so she had better be alert to his cunning. I told her: "forewarned is forearmed." She just looked at me with a blank stare and said, "What?" I didn't know if she was ready for Baxter.

His Spitfire roared into the parking lot, and Baxter came bouncing into the apartment. He was so happy to be done with his summer camp that he didn't even notice Katie in the kitchen when he came through the door. He was uncharacteristically foul with his language describing his two weeks in graphic style. I figured he'd notice Katie soon enough so I let him hang himself a little while longer. When he finally spotted her in the kitchen, he turned on his sophisticated switch and became Mr. Cool.

"Who's this?" he started. "I'm Baxter. Where did you come from? I see you've been busy while I've been gone, Sean!" He suddenly remembered his language when he came through the door and started to apologize.

"Don't worry about it," Katie said. "I've heard worse in the dorm."

After learning that she was a nurse, Baxter immediately asked if she had any friends that looked like her. He said he loved nurses and thought they were the most special people in the world. The bull was flying and Katie was still holding her own. I was beginning to wonder if I underestimated her. When Katie excused herself, Baxter couldn't wait to ask me how this all happened. He said if he were home, he could have been the one she was with. He thought they were perfect for each other. "You'll screw it up", he said laughingly, "and then I'll be there to pick up the pieces."

"Remember the roommate code," I reminded him.

I was glad Baxter approved of Katie. In spite of his protestations, he was happy I found someone I liked. When Katie came back in the room, she said she had to go but invited both of us to her place for Lasagna the following night. Before I could accept, Baxter told her he would be glad to come. Then he added, "If Sean doesn't want to, I'll come by myself."

I assured her I would be there. "Forewarned," I said.

She laughed and nodded. "Now I know what you mean."

I made sure Baxter saw me kiss Katie good-bye. He was shaking his head in disbelief when I rejoined him in the living room.

"I leave for a couple of days and you meet someone like her. How unlucky am I?" He was still shaking his head when he went into his room.

Before long Bill showed up and the two of them shared a joint. Bill was laughing as usual when he topped off the evening with shot of tequila. "Well", he said. "Is anything new around here?"

Baxter pointed at me and said: "Why don't you ask him?" And then as he turned toward me, he added in his own inimitable way: "You'll screw it up!"

## Chapter Twenty-Seven

### A NIGHT ON THE TOWN

"HI, RICH. IT'S Pat. Remember me. I'm your sister."

Pat was the only person in existence that still called me by my real name. For some reason, I didn't mind although I hated the name. The fact that she sarcastically ask if I remembered her was to remind me how long it had been since we last talked. I thought about her often but my life had become an egocentric world which didn't leave any room for looking back. It had been several years since her wedding and she now had two small boys. I was suddenly feeling guilty about not seeing her for a while.

"Hello, Pat," I said apprehensively. "Are you mad at me for not calling home lately?"

"No," she said. "I just needed to talk to my brother."

"Something wrong?" I could sense from her hesitation that there was a problem.

"Well...don't get too upset but Gary and I are getting divorced. He moved out last week. The boys and I are going to stay in the house until we sell it and then move to a smaller place."

I couldn't believe what I was hearing. I knew things were less than perfect from news reports I got from June. Gary was drinking way too much and Pat was close behind. The pressures of a young family and a big mortgage were taking their toll. But, I never thought they'd split. They were the class couple for God's sake!

"Is this final? Do you want me to talk to him?" I briefly thought about my head getting squeezed again, which I know would be even worse if he were drinking.

"Talking's over," she said. "It's a mutual decision."

"What about the kids?"

"They're fine. Mom's helping me. Believe me they're better off not having to listen to the arguments all the time."

"Is there anything I can do?"

"Well...how would you like a couple of guests for the weekend. Sue told me a trip to Boston was just the medicine I needed. She told me to call to see if we could stay with you. It's ok if you say no."

Sue had been Pat's friend for years. One thing about my sister, she attracted loyal and lifelong friends. This would be the first time any of my family had even seen where we lived. I knew Pat had never been to Boston, and I was anxious to show her all the historical sights and all the hot spots.

"Come on up. Baxter and I will be your personal tour guides."

Pat's visit was a big deal for me. My emotions were being pulled in every direction. On one hand I was happy in the relationship that was blossoming with Katie, but extremely dismayed by Pat's pending divorce. My job at NASA was going well except for the rumors of future job insecurity. 1972 was a presidential election year and if Nixon was re-elected, there was a chance that NASA could be moved to a more Republican friendly state. Anti-American sentiment was spreading across the country triggering riots and chaos. It was a tough time to be a conservative, riot control trained, short haired, card carrying member of the National Guard living among the student population of Boston. In spite of all my emotional swings, I was really looking forward to Pat's visit.

The girls showed up on Friday evening. Baxter and I decided to take them to the Point After, which was located downtown. The Point was once our favorite nightclub where there were always famous athletes hanging around the bar. Gino Cappelletti, the former kicker for the New England Patriots owned the bar, and his waitressing staff wore nothing but his number 20-football jersey and white boots. Gino's taste in waitresses was exquisite and their good looks drew many young eligible guys to the bar. We thought Pat and Sue would enjoy the atmosphere. Neither had ever been to a bar with this many beautiful people. Pat told me we made a great choice. Almost immediately they both noticed the handsome dark haired guy that came in wearing a knee length light brown leather jacket with matching beautiful girls on each arm.

"Who's that, Sean?" Sue wanted to know. I told her that was Derek Sanderson who played for the Bruins. "He usually has more than two girls with him. It must be a slow night!"

After a couple hours rubbing elbows with the rich and obnoxious, we took the girls to one of our neighborhood bars in Brighton. The drinks were cheaper, the clientele was more normal and the ambiance more relaxed. You could see that the girls were far more comfortable in this environment. We ran into some friends and everyone sat around and had a good time. I know Pat came with a heavy heart but she was relaxed and having fun. As often happened on our nights out, we invited a bunch of people back to the apartment after last call at the bar. Around three o'clock in the morning, everybody was hungry. I agreed to go out to the all night convenience store and buy some eggs and bacon. When I got back to the apartment, Pat took over and cooked breakfast for all 12 of the people who were still around. Bill and Larry thought it was the best breakfast they ever had and everyone else was extremely complimentary.

"You see, Pat," I said to her in private. "Life goes on and now you're already an honorary Bostonian."

The night ended around four o'clock. The girls went to sleep and slept until noon. Although still a tad hung over, they helped clean up the mess from the previous night and then said their goodbyes. Before they left, Pat gave me a big hug and said it was just what she needed. "That makes two of us", I responded. "Remember, you can come back anytime."

"I can see why you love it here, Rich," she said, "but try to come home once in a while. Mom and Dad would love to see you. By the way, they told me to say that."

It was great seeing my sister. Even though it wasn't under the best of circumstances, she had a great time. She left me with a clear message—I still had a family at home. I would try in the very near future to no longer take that fact for granted.

# Chapter Twenty-Eight

## MAN'S BEST FRIEND

THE RUMOR MILL was grinding overtime at work. President Nixon had not only won the 1972 election, his victory was one of the most lopsided in history. Just months before the election, Nixon's chance of winning seemed to be slipping away with the nightly news stories of our setbacks in Vietnam. However, two weeks before the election, Secretary of State, Henry Kissinger, announced that "peace was at hand." As a result, an unpopular incumbent won 49 out of the 50 states. Unfortunately for us, Massachusetts was the lone state to vote against him. As government contractors working in a federal building, we had no idea of the ramifications of this lone dissenting vote.

President Nixon was unflatteringly called, "Tricky Dick", because he was a paranoid, vindictive man who believed in identifying his enemies and punishing them. He perceived the people of Massachusetts to be his enemies and he threatened to punish the entire state by closing all the federal government facilities, including NASA. Suddenly my job and those of a very effective group of workers were in jeopardy. After weeks working in limbo, the axe fell with the announcement that NASA was moving its entire operation to another state. In spite of my quick rise from Xerox boy to editor, I was about to be unemployed.

Help from a familiar source rode in on a white horse just in the nick of time. The current Secretary of Transportation and former Governor of Massachusetts, John Volpe came to the aid of his former state and brought a branch of the U.S. Department of Transportation to Cambridge to take over the NASA building. My job and the jobs of most of my co-workers were saved. The only thing that really changed for our contract group was working for a different acronym. DOT didn't convey the glamorous image of NASA, but it was certainly better than unemployment. Unfortunately, my mentor and colleague, Frank Lynn, was a victim of the change when he was asked to retire. I would miss him. I was now the lead editor, but consistent with the wage freeze, my income remained the same. They were, in my humble opinion, getting a hell of a bargain.

It had been several months since my first date with Katie and the novelty hadn't even begun to disappear. I had met her entire family at one time when we went for Thanksgiving at her parent's house in Beverly. A few days before, I had surprised Katie with an adorable blonde Cocker Spaniel puppy named Goldie. Neither of us felt comfortable leaving little Goldie alone for the whole day so we brought her with us. What seemed like a good idea to help me break the ice with her family, backfired. Just as we arrived, Goldie got all excited about stopping somewhere and peed all over my lap. I had to face the inquisition of the curious relatives with puppy pee covering the front of my pants. To us it was a funny moment and actually eased any tension that might have existed. I guess the family decided I couldn't be that bad if I handled the situation with good humor rather than getting mad at the dog. Meeting more than thirty people at once was traumatic, but thanks to Goldie running interference for me, the day went well. Katie was the prize of the family, and I had to pass muster to be deemed worthy. It was becoming obvious that our relationship was taking steps in a direction that I didn't think I would go again. Sometimes we don't have control of these things.

Not everyone was happy with Katie and me spending Thanksgiving in Beverly. The next day I received an angry call at the apartment. It was June.

"Are you ever coming home," she started. "Your mother's very upset. You know how much Thanksgiving has always meant to her. Your absence was painfully obvious."

She went on and on about my lack of feelings for my family and my selfishness. She stopped only after saying she would come to Boston herself and drag me back by the ear if that's what it took. I knew from previous experience how painful that could be, so I was reluctant to upset her any further.

"I'll be there next weekend," I told her. "I'm bringing my girlfriend to meet you and the rest of the family. Oh, and my little puppy's coming, too. Tell Mom that the puppy is mostly house broken so she won't worry about her new rugs."

June finally calmed down and said she would look forward to it. She said Dad's got a surprise for you too. I wondered what that could be. I also wondered how I was going to housebreak Goldie in a couple of days.

# Chapter Twenty-Nine

## A KNIGHT IN KING ARTHUR'S COURT

THE PARIS PEACE Accord was signed in January of 1973 effectively ending our participation in the Vietnam War. President Nixon, however, had more problems at home. As the result of the Watergate Break-In and resultant cover up, he was under the threat of being impeached from office. While the world teetered on the brink of insanity, Katie and I continued our relationship.

Katie had become a regular in our group. She was always in a good mood and the guys, including Larry and Bill, liked her a lot. Bill's wife felt more comfortable hanging around with us now that a girl was part of the pack, a fact that really curtailed Bill's drug use. Larry's wife was hardly ever seen even though they had moved into Dale and Maureen's apartment directly below us when the girls had been assigned to another city. Larry was best described as an odd duck. He would act like one of the guys and then withdraw into a strange mode of conversation where you almost felt like you were being interviewed. He had a superiority complex that at times was infuriating. Sometimes I thought to myself that he was very nosey about other people's business. He played and interacted with us, and drank with us; but, I never saw him drink too much and he never used any drugs or smoked any of Bill's cigarettes. My intuition proved correct one morning when Larry's wife came to our door and was crying uncontrollably.

"Larry leaves every morning for work at the accountant firm," she sobbed. "Today I called and they told me that nobody by

that name ever worked there. I have no idea what's going on."
She was now hysterical in her sobbing as she described their life
together. "For two years he's left here wearing a suit for a job he
doesn't even have. Why has he been lying to me? I can't believe
this is happening!"

She said she found a pile of rent checks in his desk drawer
unused. She went over to see the apartment manager who lived
in the next building and asked about the rent and all he would
say was you had better ask your husband. We were all astonished
and baffled by this whole scene.

Larry didn't come home that evening and his wife was mum
concerning his whereabouts. Within a couple of days they had
moved out. Bill, who knew Larry best, was as dumbfounded as
we were. Bits and pieces of information came out in the next few
days and finally we were able to deduce what really happened.
Larry was an undercover operative who was working for our
paranoid government. He was sent to live and coexist with the
young people of Boston to view first hand the motives and actions
of the suspected subversive culture. He was living rent free and
the operation was so secretive that not even his wife was allowed
to know. Baxter panicked when he found out about Larry because
he thought he was the target of his observations.

"I'm dead meat," he said. "Larry knows everything about me.
He knows I do drugs and sometimes give pills to girls. He's going
to nail me."

"Baxter, listen to me." I said. "You're small potatoes compared
to what they'd be looking for. They're targeting subversives and
counter culture radicals. They want theleaders of the youthful
rebellion in this country. They're after the draft dodgers and the
idiots who are burning the American flag and denigrating our
country. The only person you're leading astray is Bill and only
because he's willing. Larry is not after us. If he was, we would have
been sent away a long time ago." Baxter was still uneasy.

All I could think of was that Nixon was a piece of work. His
methods of operation included spying and eavesdropping on the

private lives of free citizens. As our president, he had violated every civil liberty granted to us under the Constitution of the United States. His reign of terror thankfully ended in August of 1974 when he resigned the presidency rather than face impeachment.

All of a sudden it seemed like there was never a dull moment at Chandler Pond. Katie and I thought that this would be a good time to visit my family for the second time. Our first visit was cut short by Goldie pooping on my mom's new rug. This time Baxter said he would watch the dog so we could stay the weekend. God knows what was in store for poor Goldie, but Baxter loved her as much as we did, so we were cautiously optimistic that he would take good care of her. Goldie was such a sweetheart and had been a great addition to our lives.

On the way down to Connecticut, Katie pressed me on why I never told her that I loved her. I said I had been badly hurt before and was being careful this time. She said that she loved me and it would be nice if I reciprocated. I told her she was very lovable. I just needed more time. Even though I hadn't used the "L" word, we would still have conversations about our future together. The most important thing was that she definitely wanted children. And thinking back to Rick's advice about picturing the girl as the mother of your kids, it was easy to picture Katie in that role. Yes, there was little doubt that I loved her, but I was still having trouble saying it.

# Chapter Thirty

## THE ROAD NOT TAKEN

THE ARRIVAL AT my parent's home was more of a big deal than we could have imagined. It seemed every relative in my family tree was there to greet us and, presumably, to judge Katie. In short order she won everybody over. Girls like her come along only once in a while and it was great that she was universally accepted. I could tell by my mother's contented smile that she thought Katie was great and a good match for me. Even Pat, who could have been potentially her biggest critic, got along famously with her from the very beginning. The last stumbling block might have been Rick who had that innate intuition about whether someone was real and not just putting on a fake front. I could tell that he approved when he went into his Mr. Charming role and hugged her. She had passed inspection.

The last time we visited, cut short by the Goldie incident, hadn't allowed anytime to talk to my father about what June had said was a surprise. He seemed reluctant or even afraid to talk to me. It was so unlike him to be reticent about expressing himself to any of his kids. It was almost awkward because I could tell he wanted to say something. Finally, I said to him: "Dad, did you want to talk to me about something?" He hesitated for a moment and then answered, "Yes I do. Would you like to go for a quick ride with me?"

We drove only a short distance to the main highway that linked our town to Hartford in the middle of the state. He drove onto the highway and immediately pulled into a lot where there was some new construction. He stopped in front of the building and said this was going to be the new Cassidy Motors. After years of refusing to build a new facility, he had agreed to the manufacturer's request to relocate from the tiny, one car showroom that had existed since the 1940's. I wondered why at his age he had decided to assuage the representatives from Chevrolet. I was about to find out.

"Do you want a tour?"

"Sure," I said.

It was a beautiful, new facility with a multi-car showroom, a six bay service area that had plenty of room for future expansion, a fully equipped body shop complete with the latest paint booth and frame straightener, and a huge area for parts where conceivably Chip could hide. The location, right on Route 6, one of the busiest roads in eastern Connecticut, seemed ideal.

"The place looks great, Dad," I said thinking he was looking for my opinion. "I don't think you can miss here. It should be great for business."

"How's your job going?" he suddenly asked.

I responded with the now familiar refrain, "Great, except for Nixon's wage freeze."

"You know this whole business could be yours someday."

The offer came very unexpectedly. I was actually floored. We had never talked about me working in the car business. It wasn't something I ever wanted to do. I didn't know how to respond.

"Wow," I finally said. "I didn't expect you to say that. I don't know what to..."

"Before you answer, I want you to think about it. I can tell that you and Katie are serious and maybe this is the right time to consider coming into the business. Take a week or so, but let me know. Chevrolet has already said there would be no problem getting you on the ownership papers."

I told him I would think about the offer and get back to him as soon as I could. I promised I would give it serious consideration and not make a hasty decision. I wondered how Katie would like living in Danville. Boston was a hypnotic place to live; she had all her nursing buddies living there; and it was a lot closer to her hometown of Beverly. I thought about the journey my life had taken. There were many curves in the road and many detours. I didn't regret the experiences of the past, but I regretted the direction I sometimes wrongly chose. I realized that each mistake and each failed venture helped shape the person I had become. I had grown up a great deal since I first moved to Boston. Baxter and I had sought adventure and we had found it. Our lives had been full of exciting discoveries and wondrous encounters with a world we had only dreamed about. We had made scores of new friends and experienced countless unforgettable moments. At that time in my life, I couldn't imagine living in a more interesting or exciting place. Now I was being asked to consider leaving Boston for good and returning to the quiet of my hometown. I was heading full speed toward the crossroad of decision. It was going to be an interesting ride home.

We enjoyed the rest of our weekend visit. Neither my father nor I mentioned our conversation to anybody. It was great seeing everyone, but now we had to go home to Boston, home to Baxter and Goldie, home to our lives that existed before this weekend. Katie and I talked on the way back about everything except the offer. I wasn't sure how she was going to react to that especially if it meant separating for a while.

Two days, three days, four days went by and I still hadn't made up my mind about anything. I woke up the next morning with a plan. It would be interesting to see if it worked.

That night, I took Katie to a Red Sox game. She wasn't a big fan but liked to go to Fenway Park for the experience. We were sitting in the left field grandstands when my favorite player, Carl Yastrzemski, came to the plate. He was going through his pre-batting routine when I leaned over to her and whispered: "Katie, I love you. Will you marry me?" She was speechless with her mouth wide open—but only for a minute. She started to excitedly answer in a positive way when I told her to please wait until Yaz was done batting. I thought she was going to explode waiting, but fortunately, Yaz got a hit on the first pitch. She gave me a big hug and said yes. She then proceeded to tell everyone around us that we had just gotten engaged. Our section of fans started to applaud and offer their congratulations. It was a moment neither of us would ever forget.

With the Fenway proposal out of the way, it was time to tell Baxter. We went straight home from the ball park. Baxter was napping on the couch with Goldie in his arms. We hated to break up this cute little scene but Katie couldn't wait any longer. "We're getting married," she blurted out. Baxter woke up and she repeated her news.

"How'd the Sox do?" Baxter asked as if nothing had changed. He then laughed and said: "You mean he didn't blow it after all. You know, Katie, it's not too late to change your mind. I'm still available."

Katie would have none of it. She quickly went into the other room to call her parents and everyone else she knew. One thing for sure, there was no doubt about her answer.

When Baxter and I were alone, he asked, "What are you going to do now? Are you going to take your father's offer?" I had confided in Baxter about the offer but had yet to talk to Katie about it. I told him I still hadn't made up my mind. "Well, let's open a bottle of wine and toast the two of you. You think she'll ever get off the phone long enough to join us?"

A few minutes later Katie came back and we had our toast. It was then that I said to Baxter: "You know I want you to be my best man. You think you can handle it without losing the ring?" He laughed and said it would be his honor as long as he got to kiss the bride first. "You can wait," he said. "You'll have your chance on the honeymoon." Some things never change and thank God they don't.

The next day I approached Katie with my father's offer. She didn't seem surprised, although she knew of my reluctance to go into the car business. We discussed our future; we discussed living in Boston in contrast to Connecticut; and we discussed leaving all our friends behind. Busing had become a very big issue in Boston. Integration of schools was going to be mandatory and where your kids went to school was going to be determined by the court system. Raising kids in Boston was going to take on a whole different approach to their education. We decided after a long discussion that while it would be easier just to stay in Boston, in the long run we might be better off in Connecticut. The cost of living was less. We would be able to afford a bigger and a nicer home. The pace of living and the traffic was less of a problem and the education of our kids and the choice of schools would be in our hands. Finally, the opportunity to run my own business was appealing. It was a difficult decision, but we decided to try the unknown and pray for the best. We would go back, back to my roots, to start our new life together.

*Two roads diverged in a yellow wood*

*And sorry I could not travel both*

*And be one traveler, long I stood*

*And looked down one as far as I could*

*To where it bent in the undergrowth*


*And both that morning equally lay*

*In leaves no step had trodden back.*

*Oh, I kept the first for another day!*

*Yet knowing how way leads on to way*

*I doubted if I should ever come back.*

*I shall be telling this with a sigh*

*Somewhere ages and ages hence:*

*Two roads diverged in a wood, and I...*

*I took the one less traveled by,*

*And that has made all the difference.*


*Robert Frost: The Road Not Taken*

# Chapter Thirty-One

## THE WELCOME MAT

GOING BACK CONNOTES taking a step in the wrong direction – a retreat from a higher goal. It conjures up thoughts of failure and a reverse in fortune. My going back to Danville was none of these things. I was going back by choice. I was making a rational decision to build a more stable and financially secure future where I felt most comfortable, where my roots were buried deep in solid ground.

There is, however, something very deflating about moving back home after several exciting years in the big city. You imagine that the town's people are talking about you – about how you couldn't make it in the citified air. You feel like stopping every person you see to explain why you made the decision to come back, that it had nothing to do with failure or incompetence, but rather a conscious choice to rejoin the sanity of a small rural town. You suddenly realize that a whole bunch of people know who you are. You also realize that the anonymity that you so cherished in the city was gone. You can no longer act like a fool and care less if anybody sees you. You can no longer walk down the street without someone talking to you and asking about the family or the state of the business. You can no longer meet someone and not have fifteen people tell you what's wrong with them. There are no secrets in a small town and there are no barriers. If you're in business, you have become part of the public conversation and how you act or react to your fellow citizens determines your place in society. You automatically become a mover and a shaker – like it or not – and your every move is scrutinized. The smaller the town, the more intense is the scrutiny.

Friends are different. It is their normal reaction to throw out the welcome mat and catch up on old times. You clean up your stories for the girls and spice them up for your male friends. You left several years ago with little or no fanfare, but you return with a story to tell and an audience to listen to your tales. When the American author, Thomas Wolfe, wrote that "You Can't Go Home," he no doubt was not thinking of Danville, Connecticut, for I not only came home, I came back to friends and family that seemed genuinely happy that I was back. Of course, life was going to be a great deal slower and quieter. From the bright lights of Boston to the dull streetlights of Danville, I was in for another cultural shock. I hoped that my inner clock, the same clock that never seemed to stop in Boston, could adjust to normal hours of work and sleep. In Boston, the nightlife never ended; in Danville, they rolled up the streets at ten o'clock. It was the end of August in 1974 and my father and I had just opened the new dealership on Route 6. It was a new beginning, not only for me, but also for my father and all the employees at Cassidy Motors. Change is sometimes accepted, sometimes not.

Katie stayed back in Boston. She was now living with Phyllis until June 21st of next year when we would be married. Baxter also stayed in Boston. He got another roommate from his club to share expenses, but from what I knew of this guy, I hoped Baxter didn't land in jail. Goldie stayed with Katie and provided companionship for her when she drove down to Connecticut on weekends. Without my running mate and my fiancé, I imagined life was going to be quite dull for the next few months. How wrong I was.

# Chapter Thirty-Two

## THE INDOCTRINATION

"WHERE'S THE GOLDEN boy?"

Jacques asked the question defiantly as I approached unnoticed. His audience of three mechanics and my brother, Chip, had gathered outside the parts room to discuss the anticipated appearance of the new guy in charge. Jacques was the incumbent general manager of Cassidy Motors and had expected to occupy that same position in the new dealership facility. He was obviously upset about being replaced by a very inexperienced though very cocky son of the owner. I heard his sarcastic comment but chose to ignore it, at least for the present.

"Good morning, guys," I said curtly. "There's a meeting in my office in ten minutes. Let everyone know and tell them not to be late. I don't like late."

The message had been sent. Jacques stormed off in a fury, but I knew he wouldn't dare miss the meeting. Chip hurried after me as I walked down the hall to the showroom and followed me into my new office. He warned me to watch my step because Jacques was going to be out to get me. I found it strange that my older brother was providing me with instantaneous support for he had been vocally critical of my new position. I took his warning for what it was worth and gave him no ammunition to fire in the opposite direction. Chip had become a bit of a gossip and would have taken some pleasure in stirring up a controversy. One very valuable lesson I had learned working for the government was that office politics were territorial and workers were very protective of their own turf. I knew not to trust anyone initially until they had proven their loyalty. At this point, that very much included Chip. We had grown up together, sharing the same room, yet I still wasn't certain where his allegiance lied. I was still the newcomer – the "golden boy," as Jacques described me. My first job at Cassidy Motors was to determine those employees that were going to continue their careers with us. They would have to prove to me their value and their loyalty. It was going to be an interesting first few weeks for I also had to prove myself to them.

The office my father provided me was at the far end of the showroom. It was situated in such a way that I could see most of the showroom and I also had an outside view of the west side of the building where the new car inventory was parked. I would soon learn that one person could not watch all four corners of the dealership without the assistance of some reliable workers. The problem was identifying those workers.

I was accustomed to an office with twenty secretaries in the typing pool. At Cassidy Motors, my father only had one secretary/bookkeeper, a beautiful woman from Montreal, Canada, who had moved to Danville with her two young boys following a divorce. She had only worked for my father for a couple of months, but in that short time had become indispensible. She was not only stylishly sexy, but was also one of the most competent and efficient woman I've ever met. Her manner of speaking, spiced with a lyrical French accent, could wake up the dead. She had learned the very complex Chevrolet accounting system while employed at a dealership in Montreal. It took me only a few minutes to realize that this beautiful lady named Josette would be a valuable ally. She assisted me at that first meeting and became an irreplaceable and trusted confidante. Josette met Katie soon after and the two became instant friends. There was one plus to having a beautiful woman working for you in Danville. The state troopers who were stationed in town had a network for finding attractive women. Almost daily, one of the troopers would find any of a myriad of excuses to visit the dealership. Because of Josette, I never felt so protected.

The first meeting was mostly uneventful. I established some policy rules and described in detail the new philosophy at Cassidy Motors—to attract and maintain through customer satisfaction with our sales and service, a whole new segment of the local population. For years, Danville was considered a French Canadian town. Once strictly a mill town with ethnic housing surrounding the mills, the majority of the inhabitants had come down from Canada. When I was a youngster walking to school, the predominant language being spoken on the street by the townspeople was French. It was almost like living in Quebec, and indeed, one of the more popular housing centers was called Quebec Square. My family was definitely in the minority in those days and I can remember my mother talking about being the subject of prejudice because of her German heritage. As the mills closed one-by-one, the population of the town had become more diversified. The French Canadians, however, maintained their language as a means of independence. The old dealership had been located in Quebec Square and consequently, a large percentage of the customers were French. It only made sense in those days to have French-speaking salesmen. Jacques was one of them.

As I finished my brief introduction to the policies and procedure of the future, I asked if anyone had any comments. Jacques jumped at the chance. He targeted the French-speaking workers in the office and began with an impassioned plea for unity against the new guy. His entire speech was in French and was laced with obscenities. What he didn't know was that having grown up in this town, I understood a great deal of their Canuck dialect. What I didn't understand, Josette interpreted for me after the meeting. She was embarrassed at some of the unpleasant things that were said about me but I told her not to worry. They were going to do things my way or they would be gone. She shrugged her shoulders, smiled, and said, "OK Boss!"

I knew coming into my father's business that there would be some drawbacks, but I hadn't imagined the struggle with which I was constantly confronted. The external worries centered around a lingering recession triggered by rising inflation, long gas lines, ridiculously high interest rates, high unemployment, and negative consumer confidence. Add to that a Chevrolet lineup of cars that had lost touch with the needs of the consumers, and my mission to build the business from a small corner dealership with apartments upstairs and a gas pump in front, to a modern, sophisticated operation on a major highway seemed implausible. Each morning I would leave for work with a sigh and a fear of what might go wrong that day. Each day seemed to live up to my fears.

The sales staff that my father turned over to me was a joke. Jacques was the man in charge who moved at his own pace from the showroom to the service area to the body shop. He was basically a mechanic, but possessed the ability to sell anything to anyone as long as they were numbered among his compatriots. He was crass and ill mannered and totally incapable of dealing with customers of other nationalities. When he arrived in the showroom to help with sales, he would be covered from head to toe with grease and oil. He was very secretive about his deals and his customers were suspiciously loyal.

The other salesman, Francois, was a lot less intense and much more likeable, but he, too, catered to his own people. Francois was a notorious womanizer who would disappear at the most inappropriate times to visit his latest conquest. His constant cigar smoking was creating an unhealthy environment in our new showroom, but it was tolerated because it was determined that he was actually an asset to the dealership. He possessed a charming personality that was difficult to be upset with for very long. He had a gift for selling, and he took very good care of his customers. His major drawback was that he had never learned as a schoolboy in Canada to read or write. For years, he relied on my father to take care of all his paperwork and to keep his secret of illiteracy.

That task had now fallen on my shoulders. Francois and Jacques were buddies. At least initially, they were going to do everything they could to make me fail.

I had come into the dealership presumably to manage the sales staff and increase our market penetration. My background did not include dealing with ethnic prejudices or deceitful practices. I was in for a unique and often bitter indoctrination. Internal strife and roaring inflation – what a start!

I was faced with a sales force and a client base that was disproportionate to the growing diversity in the community. My salesmen were woefully inadequate to handle the new population of the area, and I was beginning my career in the automobile business as the Irish/German devil that was being portrayed as anti-French by enemies that came with the territory. My father had lured me back from Boston with a description of being the 'big fish in the small pond'. Instead I was being thrown into a pond full of piranhas.

# Chapter Thirty-Three

## FOR BETTER OR WORSE

"HELLO, THIS IS Baxter. May I speak to Sean, please?'
Josette came to my office entrance and told me a very
polite young man was on the phone. She didn't detect Baxter's
obvious attempt to impress her. He never let an opportunity go by
to flirt with a beautiful lady. I took the call deciding not to warn
her about my buddy.

"Bax, babe. What's happening? You need some bail
money?"

"Man, what an accent your secretary has. You know how I
love accents. Maybe she could make me forget Anna."

"I think the problem is Anna has forgotten you. Besides,
you're going to have to stand in line for Josette. Every male with
a pulse in Danville is after her. And the good thing is she could
care less. She's an absolute gem and we are so lucky to have her. If
you gave up all your bad habits, which I know you won't, I might
fix you up. As you can see, I've become very protective."

"Well, there's always Katie," he laughed. "Hey, I'm coming
home this weekend. Are you going to be around or is the ball and
chain coming down?"

"Katie can't make it until Saturday. You can meet me at the
cottage on Friday and we can do something."

"I'll be there around six o'clock. See you then."

It was February. It had been six months since I moved back
from Boston and it was just four months before my impending
marriage. Our engagement had gone quite smoothly up to this

point and unless I did something stupid in the next four months, Katie and I would be married on June 21. I had rented a cottage on Lake Alexander, a beautiful fresh water lake only four miles from work, basically to separate myself from the interminable rules of my father's house. I was twenty-eight years old and needed my own space. At first, my mother made a bit of a fuss about it, but Pat intervened and convinced her that I was mature enough to stay out of trouble and was too old for a curfew. Usually when Baxter showed up, there was no need for rules because we would have broken all of them anyway. This night would not be an exception. It was good to see Baxter. We had some catching up to do.

"Did you invite Josette to join us," Baxter asked as he walked into the cottage.

"No, Baxter. Not in this lifetime. You couldn't handle her anyway. She has way too much class for you. She doesn't smoke, drinks very little, and has two young boys at home. She doesn't need to meet the devil at this stage of her life."

"Sounds boring. Maybe she could use a joint?"

"Baxter, Baxter, Baxter. Will you ever straighten out your life?"

He thought about my question for a moment and then replied, "Nah! Let's go to Providence tonight. Chubby Checker's singing at some club on the south side."

"Chubby Checker! Is he still alive? Nobody does the twist anymore."

The club that Baxter took me to on the south side of Providence was in the middle of the black section. It was a small bar with a seating capacity of about twenty-five people. I thought to myself what would Chubby Checker be doing in a dump like this? He used to be a big star. There were a couple of things that bothered me about this place. The most obvious was the fact that we were the only white people there and the club was nearly empty except for some rather scary black dudes that were giving us the eyeball. This wasn't the first time Baxter had taken me to an all black club.

The last time was in the middle of the racial riots and we were lucky to escape with our lives. I attempted to make a long distance phone call to Katie that night from the phone booth inside the bar, but was chased out of the booth by a very large black woman who was brandishing a gun. She said her call was more important and to get lost white boy before I got hurt. We left soon after that incident, but here we were again, tempting fate for the thrill of it. I wondered why I listened to him.

Chubby Checker came on stage and gave a good performance in spite of the small crowd. We enjoyed the show and later mingled with some of the patrons at the bar. Once we had convinced them that we weren't a threat, but were there just for the music, they accepted us. It turned out to be a memorable evening, in a good way, and we probably did more for racial relations that night then we realized. Baxter had no fear of these situations. He probably could have been the ambassador to the United Nations for he had that ability to get along with people of all races and nationalities. I was glad that he was my friend and that I had chosen him to be my best man. I was just hoping that we lived long enough to see my wedding day.

# Chapter Thirty-Four

## TOIL AND TROUBLE

"UNEASY LIES THE head that wears the crown." My English training at Merrimack had provided me with many historical quotes that seemed apropos for the time. Shakespeare's description of the uneasiness Henry IV experienced as the ruling monarch of England, seemed aptly descriptive of the task that lie ahead of me as the ruling dictator of Cassidy Motors. Many decisions I was forced to make were unpopular among the workers, especially the salesmen, but nonetheless, had to be made. I had always been popular in school and later in my personal life in Boston. To be suddenly reviled by the majority of my new co-workers was a development that did not set well with me. Like Henry IV, I was having a difficult time sleeping.

> "... O Sleep, O gentle Sleep.
>
> Nature's soft nurse, how have I frighted thee,
>
> That thou no more wilt weigh my eyelids down
>
> And steep my senses in forgetfulness?"
>
> William Shakespeare: Henry IV

As the days turned to weeks, it became apparent to me that I had to make some personnel changes. I had mentioned to my father several times that Jacques was not the asset he thought he was. My father didn't like to deal with the everyday problems that existed in the car business. He preferred that I handle those problems. Jacques had worked for him for over ten years and my father trusted him. In his defense, he had run the dealership during those times when Dad was incapacitated with alcohol abuse. It came to my attention, however, that his way of running the business included a rather healthy share of the profits. He worked on customer's cars in the back of the building without a written repair order. Parts were taken from the parts department without billing them and happy customers left without any record of their appointment. Other abuses were coming to light as Josette's inventory control was uncovering frequent billing irregularities. I had to confront Jacques with these concerns. His reaction was predictable.

"Don't you worry, little man," he said. "I've been in this business a long time and I know what I'm doing. Why don't you go back to your office and do what you do. By the way, what do you do?"

Instead of provoking a scene with an accusatory response, I chose to answer with a succinct reply. "Jacques, I'm afraid you may soon find out."

There's an old saying that you shouldn't engage somebody in a battle of wits if you're only half armed. I think Jacques was intelligent enough to know that he was the one without the full arsenal. He huffed off without a response.

Soon after, my father came to me and asked my impressions of my first few months in the business. I gave him a synopsis of the direction I thought the dealership had to go, and then I gave him an appraisal of how I viewed the personnel. I was obviously very complimentary of Josette and for the most part thought the mechanics were capable although limited in their training. I told him we needed to upgrade the quality of work coming out of the body shop and we needed a more diversified sales staff. I told him I thought Francois was doing a good job in spite of his few bad habits—habits of which my father was well aware. When the subject came to Jacques, my father became defensive. He said

Jacques had seen them through some tough times and he felt he owed him his endorsement. I decided it was time to peel the onion.

"Dad, he's stealing you blind. I think I've only touched the surface, but Josette and I have uncovered a large number of irregular billings that can be traced to him. He's repairing friend's cars in the back of the building and taking cash that never gets put on the books. His smugness is infuriating. He thinks you'll never find out because he doesn't think you care. I don't know how else to put it, but he's playing you for a sucker!"

"He's too valuable." he said. "You leave Jacques to me."

I couldn't leave it alone. I responded somewhat heatedly. "You've got to be kidding. He's a thief. We're going nowhere as long as he works here. Maybe it's time for me to look for another job, because I refuse to work with him."

My father wasn't one to back into a corner. I knew his Irish might come out, but I also knew what was right. It was time to move on from the Jacques' years. It was him or me.

# Chapter Thirty-Five

## THE BRIDGE OVER TROUBLED WATER

I AWOKE ON the morning of June 21st with my mind racing and my head pounding from the previous night bachelor fling that Baxter had arranged. I had told him I didn't want a bachelor party because I didn't want to be placed in a situation where I regretted my participation in some meaningless romp with a nameless dancer or, worse yet, a hooker. Katie didn't deserve that kind of behavior so I disappointed a large number of my friends and Baxter by denying them the opportunity to embarrass me one last time. I did, however, agree to go bar hopping on Route I in Danvers and Peabody with just Baxter and my nephew, Jack, who was serving as an usher at the wedding. Jack was a freshman in college and was unfamiliar with the extent to which Baxter would go to practice his devious intentions. He would soon accelerate his education by achieving a new level of improper behavior courtesy of my best man.

We started out that night without much of a game plan other than to hit as many bars on the northbound side of Route 1 as on the southbound side. Jack was attempting to hang with us, but Baxter and I were professionals at this stage of our life and drinking with us took a great deal of stamina and intestinal fortitude. After several stops, we noticed Jack was beginning to slur his speech and was wavering while he walked. His vulnerability would be exploited by Baxter at our next stop. The name of the bar was the Green Apple. It might just as well have been called the Adam's Apple for this was a drag club where all the dancers and waitresses were men dressed as women. Jack had no idea that these girls were actually men and approached an attractive transvestite and offered to buy her a drink. Baxter was in his element when he had a chance to embarrass someone. He encouraged Jack to ask the "girl" to dance. While he was dancing and attempting to be charming to impress us, Baxter and I left and went to the next bar. After we stopped laughing, we went back to the Green Apple to see if Jack had "scored." Jack was noticeably disturbed when we returned proclaiming much too loudly for our safety, "Did you know these girls were men. These girls are men!" he repeated. Baxter and I decided for his own well being that we should get Jack out of there before he was thrown out. He made us swear that we would never tell anyone at the wedding about the Green Apple and then he threw up. Jack's night was over so we took him back to his motel room. He made it to the wedding the next morning, but maintained a sheepish look throughout the day. Baxter had struck again.

It was three o'clock in the morning when my best man and I returned to the motel where most of our friends were staying and were already asleep. We both decided to get something to eat and went across the street to an all night diner. This would be our last conversation as single buddies who five years before set out on our great adventure to the big city of Boston. In biblical terms, this was our last supper.

Baxter said he was happy for Katie and me but wished we could start over again and eliminate all our mistakes. I told him that would take all the fun out of the adventure for mistakes are what made the last five years interesting.

"Do you wish that you had never met Anna?" I asked.

"No, but I wish I hadn't blown it with her. I still think of her all the time. She'll be tough to replace."

"Well, you know the tough time I went through with Alix. I felt just like you did about Anna, but then Katie kind of dropped into my life and I guess that's the way it was meant to happen.

Somebody will come along to take Anna's place and it will all be just a sweet memory."

"I hope you're right because all I'm meeting these days are bimbos and barflies. I hope my chance of finding a nice girl hasn't passed me by."

"Maybe you ought to change a few things in your life. Get out of the city for a while. Come back to Danville. You wouldn't believe how the selection of good - looking girls has improved since we left. There ought to be one around somewhere that would take pity on you."

"Maybe you're right. By the way, are you still going through with this wedding? We're only a couple hours from Canada. You could call her from there and say you got cold feet. I'm sure it wouldn't take her long to get over you. You're kind of forgettable."

I knew Baxter was only kidding but the hours were dwindling before the wedding and my feet were getting colder. It was four o'clock in the morning – only six hours of bachelorhood left. It was time to get some sleep. I was glad I had these last moments as a single guy with Baxter. It was fitting that our journey was ending in a beautiful place like Beverly, Massachusetts, and I was beginning the rest of my life with one of that town's nicest exports. I had gone to Boston to experience life and somehow along the way had found my life's partner. As tempting as Baxter's suggestion about Canada was, there was no way I was going to miss this wedding. At ten o'clock that morning, hung over and groggy, with Jack and Chip as ushers and Baxter as my best man, I exchanged vows with Katie. I knew that I was, indeed, the lucky one and I would try to remember that for the rest of my life.

# Chapter Thirty-Six

## THE INDY PACE CAR

GERALD FORD TOOK over for Nixon as president after Nixon resigned rather than face impeachment in August of 1974. As slippery as he sometimes seemed, Nixon made his mark in foreign affairs by opening up relations with China and entering into discussions with Russia about disarming both country's nuclear arsenals. Without the shenanigans of Watergate and his misuse of the various intelligence agencies within the government to cover up the Watergate scandal, his legacy could have been much different. New President Ford was the right man at the time to heal a nation's wounds. He would finish the remaining two and a half years of Nixon's aborted presidency. With the chaos that our country had gone through, it was a difficult time to be in business.

My problems with Jacques had come to a head. He lobbied in French for Josette to take his side, but she had already decided where her allegiance was. He huddled with various mechanics trying to undermine my growing base of support and he even struck out with Francois who knew more about the questionable activities that Jacques was engaged in than anyone else. Francois admitted to me and my father that work was being done in the back of the building by Jacques and that he was pocketing the money without billing the customers, all of whom were his friends. Finally, my father admitted that Jacques had to go.

I called Jacques into my office and informed him that we were aware of his activities and that we had decided to dismiss him.

Because of his many years of service to the dealership, we would not bring charges against him for criminal malfeasance. I told him to leave with dignity and without any rancor. He, of course, denied he had anything to do with the accusations that were being levied against him by several sources, but decided it would be best if he just left. He did provide a parting shot, however, as he warned, "Be careful, little man. Your day is coming." It would be the first of many threats that I received over the years. Such was the nature of the automobile business.

With Jacques' departure, an era at Cassidy Motors had come to an end. Hopefully, we could now proceed without conflict and without internal strife. I had to move fast to find suitable replacements for a man who had worn many hats at Cassidy's, but who unfortunately, had worn out his welcome as well with his contradictory behavior. Preparedness was my specialty and within a week I had hired two new young and enthusiastic salesmen and a new service manager. We were reloading and we were ready to take on the competition. Within months our sales had doubled and our profitability had increased. My father was noticeably pleased, although typically he never voiced his approval. We were, however, working on borrowed time.

In 1977, Jimmy Carter was elected president and it was as if someone shut the door on prosperity. Along with the entire country, we tumbled back into a spiraling recession. Soon there was double-digit inflation, double-digit unemployment, double-digit interest rates, and a burgeoning energy crisis. Selling cars became a monumental task with many hurdles to overcome. Our sales plummeted and red ink filled the books. Carter didn't seem to have a clue how to fix the problems of the economy. Consumer confidence was at an all time low. It was urgent that we had to do something.

At the beginning of the 1978 new car season, Chevrolet came out with a Twenty-Fifth Anniversary Corvette Indianapolis 500 Pace Car. Everyone of the over six thousand Chevrolet dealers in the country were to get at least one of these slick looking, limited edition models. Despite the economic turmoil, the Pace Car was a huge hit with sports car enthusiasts who were willing to spend way over the list price of the car for this instant classic. The dealers who received the car first were making large profits. Of course, we were one of the last in the area to receive the car and by the time we got it, the buzz had waned considerably. The car sat in our showroom for three months while we heard and read about the demand for the car in other parts of the country. My father wanted to sell the car wholesale to another dealer to get it off our wholesale floor planning charges. I told him that was not an option. We would sell the car. It was our first disagreement as co-owners, and I knew we were subject to a time frame that precluded my grand scheme. The pressure was on, and it was inevitable that if the car wasn't sold quickly, his intention to let the car go at a wholesale price would prevail. We had to come up with a way to make the kind of money on the car that other dealers were making. It had been three years since I first stepped into the dealership and in my mind I had yet to use my promotional skills to market the product in a profitable way. I viewed myself as somewhat of a failure in that I hadn't done enough to distance our dealership from our competition. We were too generic – too vanilla. I had to spice it up and create a unique identity. As I was lying sleepless in bed that night, I had what I thought was a great idea. I couldn't wait until morning to pitch the idea to my father. I was confident, at least outwardly, that he would be receptive.

The next morning Josette noticed a new bounce and exuberance to my step. For once, I had actually gotten a good night's sleep. I was refreshed and revved up. My father came in a bit later and also noticed a new energy in the showroom. He asked Josette what was wrong with me, and she told him that I was bubbling over with a new idea. He sarcastically stated that he couldn't wait to hear this one.

I sat my father down and simply said, "Dad, we're going to have a Corvette Raffle. It's going to be for charity and it's going to be the biggest thing to ever hit this area."

He looked at me like I had three heads and said. "OK. How are you going to pull this off?"

"We're going to raffle the Pace Car and our other new Corvette. The cost of the two cars is about twenty-two thousand dollars. We're going to sell only two hundred tickets and the tickets are going to be for two hundred dollars each. If we sell out, and I don't believe that will be a problem even in this economy, we'll split eighteen thousand dollars with our charity. That's more than we made in six months last year. Screw the recession. Let's do this!"

He looked at me for what seemed like an eternity and then said, "Go for it. But I'll be the first one to tell you I told you so if you fail."

"Failure is not an option," I responded with just a hint of cockiness.

To ensure the success of my first huge promotion, I knew every detail of the raffle would have to be first-class with no screw-ups. There would be close scrutiny from a great deal of people and even a small percentage of those were wishing I would fail. Raffle tickets had to be printed, invitations to the drawing had to be sent, and planning for the drawing in the showroom had to be inclusive for even the most minute details. The tickets were printed first and then the selling began. To my pleasant surprise, Francois had a true gift for selling raffle tickets. Within a couple of days we hit the break-even point. The interest was astounding. We were getting calls from all over the state and into Rhode Island. It was soon apparent that the demand was going to far outweigh the number of tickets. In two weeks we had sold them all. Our charity, the local ambulance fund, was ecstatic. Francois, who from then on I dubbed 'the world's greatest raffle ticket salesman,' sold over a hundred tickets himself. The personnel in the dealership and the people in town got caught up in the excitement and were anxious to find out who would be the winners of the two Corvettes. The local radio station and local newspapers soon got into the act and were giving us a great deal of publicity. I knew that we were hitting a promotional homerun that I would be remiss in not turning into an even bigger circus – one that would bring the name of Cassidy Motors into the spotlight and establish us as a place to consider when purchasing a new car or truck. The only details left were for the actual day of the drawing. The event had to live up to the hype.

I contacted a friend of mine at the high school who was involved in the cheerleading program and asked if the girls would like to participate on the day of the drawing. Danville's cheerleading squad had just been chosen one of the top groups in the state and one of the girls had been selected as an All-American and would be making an appearance at the Hula Bowl in Hawaii. The cheerleaders would add a youthful exuberance to the day plus all their relatives and friends would want to come and see them. I also contacted the Barbizon School of Modeling in Providence and hired a pair of models to work the floor as hostesses. The final touch was contacting the agent for the reigning Miss Connecticut to see if she would like to be linked to such a worthy cause in a section of the state that rarely is graced by state pageant winners. She readily accepted. Our invited guests included members of the Town Council, the Chamber of Commerce, the Board of Education, and as many dignitaries and celebrities as we could contact. We purchased two-dozen bottles of champagne and hired a local caterer to supply finger foods and hors d'oeuvres. Our planning was complete and the day was set.

The crowd that showed up for the drawing was impressive. Anyone with a ticket was certainly there and those that were just curious piled into our suddenly very crowded showroom. Miss Connecticut arrived and she was pleasant and stunning. We decided that she would draw the winning tickets from the drum that was being guarded by a pair of muscular state policemen. The models roamed around with the champagne and the cheerleaders took care of distributing the catered food. The head of the Town Council came in just before the drawing and congratulated my father on such a well-planned and successful day. Dad was beaming. The actual drawing was suspenseful and dramatic. The two winners couldn't believe their luck and displayed the expected, emotional reaction to make the moment even more exciting. The day was an overwhelming and profitable success.

When the crowd dissipated, the salesmen were suddenly inundated with new customer leads. The ambulance people were thrilled with their check for nine thousand dollars and, although he never said it, I knew my father was pleased with me. In spite of the many years that had gone by since those days when I wished he would stay home rather than embarrass me on the baseball field, I still felt compelled to try to impress my father. For one day at least, I had been successful.

# Chapter Thirty-Seven

## OUR HOUSE

ONE OF THE perks that accompanied the rapid growth of our dealership was the success we achieved in the annual Chevrolet sales contests. Most of the winners of these contests enjoyed fully paid vacations to some of the most exotic places on earth. Sales were based on performance against a sales objective. Because our objectives were relatively low – a result of our sales history at the old facility prior to our move to the new building, it was almost an annual right of passage for us to win these contests against dealerships of comparable size. Katie and I enjoyed all expense trips to Europe, Hawaii, the Caribbean Islands, Palm Springs, California, and other destinations too numerous to mention. One such trip was a spring jaunt to Las Vegas where we were to stay at the fabulous MGM Grand Hotel. This particular trip comes to mind, not only for the exciting things that happened on the trip, but also for what happened at home while we were gone.

It was the spring of 1978 and Katie was seven months pregnant with our first child. She debated for a time whether she was up to travelling, but decided to go at the last minute when she realized that I needed a vacation to relieve the stress of the business. It would be our first time in Vegas and it certainly lived up to its reputation. We both loved going to concerts and shows and were fortunate enough to get great seats to see both Glen Campbell and Ricky Nelson. The concerts were fantastic. Neither of us gambled so we spent little time in the casinos. We did, however, do all the touristy things like going to the Hoover Dam and boating on Lake Meade. In spite of her tendency to tire at an early hour we had a great time. Our last night in Vegas, Katie was pooped at eight o'clock. She told me to go down to the casino if I wanted and she would just rest in bed. I put up a feeble argument although I really wanted to go. She kissed me good night and off I went. I didn't know what to expect but I was interested in seeing what really goes on in Vegas. The volume of noise surprised me. Combined with the annoying fluorescent lights flickering in all directions and the disgusting smell of cigarettes, I quickly became disenchanted with life on the casino floor. I decided to take a walk outside down the main boulevard that splits the magnificent hotels. I imagined that on this very street walked Sinatra and Dean Martin, Bob Hope and Ann Margaret. I pictured the other greats of show business performing at various clubs along the strip. I stopped for a moment to toss a coin in an outside fountain to wish my unborn child a happy life and then I just sat and admired the spectacular architecture.

Before long I was approached by a hauntingly beautiful girl dressed in provocative clothing and wearing more lipstick than I've ever seen on one person. She smiled through her red stained lips and asked if I wanted some company. My initial instinct was to dismiss her rudely, but I decided it was a beautiful night and I could at least be pleasant. I told her I was just out for a walk and appreciated her concern, but I was just fine.

"I'm going to be a father in two months," I said. My wife is asleep in our room and I just came out to get some fresh air and enjoy your beautiful city."

"It is beautiful, isn't it? Sometimes when you live here you forget to take the time to appreciate it."

You could tell that she sensed that I wasn't going to be a customer, but she stayed around anyway and continued our chat. She asked where I was from and was excited to hear I was from Connecticut because she had applied to college there.

"You're a college student?" I asked, trying not to be too surprised.

"Yes. I'm in my third year at UNLV. I'm studying fashion design. Right now I'm working for tuition."

I didn't know what else to say. There was a time, not too long ago, when I would have welcomed the opportunity to attempt to rehabilitate this girl. She used to be my type – flashy and sensuous, but the direction of my life had changed for the better since I met Katie and my priorities had definitely changed. So I excused myself saying I had to go check on my wife. Pleasantly, almost like a tour guide, she told me she hoped I enjoyed the rest of my stay in Vegas and knew I would truly enjoy being a father. Before walking off, I felt compelled to tell her she was a very beautiful girl and I hoped she would find another way to earn a living.

"Some day maybe I'll meet someone like you and live happily ever after." She blew me a kiss as we parted ways, two strangers exchanging pleasantries on a gorgeous evening – one going back to realty and his pregnant wife and the other walking a street that might not lead to the promise land. I wished her well and went back to the casino.

The sounds of the slot machines greeted my re-entry into the MGM Grand. I decided to wander over to a side bar where just a few patrons and weary gamblers were taking a respite from the chaos and enjoying a late night drink along with the sounds of a pretty entertaining backroom band. I ordered a bourbon on the rocks and sat back to enjoy the music. This wasn't your run-of-the-mill novelty band. This band could play and the lead singer was fabulous. I sat there mesmerized. Finally I asked the waitress who this band was. She said they were called something like 'Huey Lewis and the Newspapers'. I hadn't heard of them, but it was my guess they would be famous someday. I would have to remember their name.

That night, our last night on the trip, I had spent a couple of hours alone in Vegas, had met a professional girl who just wanted to chat, and had listened to a band that was unknown to me at that time, but was as good as any band I had ever heard. My love of city life had been rekindled and my abhorrence of gambling and gamblers had been reinforced. In two hours wandering around in the city, I had experienced more than I would in two months in Danville; but I knew that my future was in a small town and my pregnant wife was going to be the center of it. I returned to my room and prepared for our trip home.

We arrived back in Connecticut on late Sunday afternoon. We were both tired from the flight and anxious to sleep in our own bed. We were unpacking when the phone rang. It was Mom. She wanted to tell us before anyone else could that they had sold the house on Broad Street. They were moving to Brooklyn, to a smaller house with a big yard. She said she didn't want to upset me, but the deal was already done. The house on Broad Street, the home where I grew up and shared so many moments with my family, was sold. I said goodbye to Mom and went into a jetlag trance. I put Katie to bed with a kiss and sat down in my reclining chair. Memories were pouring from my soul.

Eighty-one Broad Street. The address would exist in my consciousness for the rest of my life. There were so many great memories that were running through my mind as I settled into a restless slumber. The cellar came to mind first for it was there that Pat and I spent so much time together either roller skating around the ping-pong table, playing hide and seek with our friends, or spying on my sister June's high school parties. We would cleverly sneak down the stairs to the first landing and hide behind the petition. Dancing and kissing and even some drinking were secrets that we promised June we would take to our graves after we were caught spying. She laughed when we were caught and promised us that someday we would have a turn entertaining our friends and she would be there spying on us. Other cellar memories included many heated ping-pong games with Chip that usually ended in some kind of an argument. My father's contribution to the cellar memories included the infamous boat-building caper that began as an attempt to involve Chip and I in an activity with him that the three of us could enjoy together. Dad had purchased a 'Build it Yourself' kit that included hundreds of pieces of wood and screws and other essentials needed to build your own row boat. It also included detailed instructions that seemed to be written in some foreign language.Chip's participation lasted about two days before he and my father disagreed on something insignificant and began shouting at each other. Chip was banished from the project, much to his delight. That left me and Dad and a whole bunch of pieces of wood to assemble. I persevered for about two weeks before I came up with some lame excuse that my baseball coach didn't want me damaging my hands during baseball season. My father stubbornly worked on the project alone and somehow, after months of hammering and sawing, the boat was finished. We all congratulated him on his achievement and he was smugly accepting the plaudits when we attempted to remove the boat from the cellar through the bulkhead. It didn't fit the opening – not even close. Exasperated, Dad just left the freshly finished boat in the cellar and walked upstairs. The boat remained on the cellar floor for years, a symbol of my father's ingenuity.

My mind flashed to the first floor of the house where the family gathered on Sunday nights in the sunroom where our black and white television brought us the weekly story of Lassie and the entertainment of Ed Sullivan. The room was always cold in the winter so we would all huddle together on the couches under blankets and eat popcorn. I loved Sunday nights because everyone was always there as a family sharing some golden moments. Next to the sunroom was the formal living room. Against the back wall was the fireplace bordered on both sides by trophy cases filled with my father's diving trophies. It was in this room that we would always put our Christmas tree and it was in this room that my father chased his imaginary mice up the wall. Through good times and bad, it was the centerpiece of the house.

Down the hall from the living room was the entry to the kitchen where my mother practiced her culinary skills. I can still picture her in her glory preparing some glorious meal for her family. She was an artist at work. It was also in the kitchen where the Andersons and my parents would go to enjoy their highballs and sing their harmonious songs. Across the front entry way adjacent to the living room was the swinging door that opened to the dining room, the room where my father put on his evening show. I will remember forever his deep voice penetrating the quiet of the evening meal with his challenging intellectual tests.

Upstairs were the four bedrooms. Chip and I were in the bedroom at the top of the stairs. This was the room where in the closet was a ladder that led to the attic. I never admitted to him or anyone else, but often at night I heard someone upstairs in the attic walking around. I would fall asleep imagining all sorts of horrible things, but would wakeup relieved that whomever was up there, remained up there. Maybe I was dreaming, but who knows?

Out our window, we could see the back yard where Chip and I would spend hours practicing my pitching skills for Little League. He would start off in a good mood, laughing and trash talking, and usually end up angry because my fastballs would bounce in the dirt in front of him and bang into his knees. His legs were always black and blue during baseball season, but to his credit, he would always agree to play catch anytime I asked. He had his shortcomings but there was no doubt that he had a big and generous heart.

Games in the side yard, explorations of the trails behind the house, climbing the apple tree in the back yard, family get-togethers, individual graduation parties, banging a rubber ball against the garage for hours, watching my sister Pat and her friend Janice master the art of hopscotch, the different family cars in the driveway, the different pets that contributed so much to our lives – these were the memories that flashed back to me as I crashed on my chair, tuckered out from our long flight home. Waking up to the realization that the only house that I truly considered my home was no longer part of the family sent me into a depressed state of mind. Maybe I was putting too much importance on the physical trappings of a house – after all houses are just walls and a roof. But to me, Eighty-one Broad Street would always be my home.

## Chapter Thirty-Eight

### THE REAGAN YEARS

THANKFULLY THE FOUR-YEAR term of Jimmy Carter ended before the dealership went out of business. Ronald Reagan took over the presidency in January of 1981. Almost immediately, business picked up and flourished throughout his eight years in office. Americans finally had a leader with whom they had a great deal of admiration and respect. President Reagan led the United States into one of its most prosperous times. From recession to prosperity to respect around the world, the confidence of the people as citizens and as consumers was palpable. These were the good times that we had long waited for at Cassidy Motors.

Dad was noticeably less stressed with the upturn in the economy. His countenance and his demeanor were much more relaxed. Business was good and profits were soaring. He spent less and less time at the dealership, showing up in the morning to open the mail and then leaving for the day, preferring to work at home in his garden. He was more than satisfied with the job I was doing, but was still reluctant to hand over complete control of the dealership. I never pushed him on this point, in spite of his promises to me when I first came back from Boston, for I felt he deserved this time to bask in the new glory of his very successful business. I held a minority share of the dealership and just figured in good time, he would fulfill his promise. What I didn't count on was his getting sick again – the cancer had come back. Cancer is a horrible disease. It knows no timetable and it knows no mercy. When he was diagnosed with a reoccurrence of his cancer, he became moody and depressed. He felt he had done everything asked of him by his doctor. He hadn't had a drink in five years. He had maintained a healthy diet and got plenty of exercise in his garden. He looked good and was optimistic about the future. Katie and I had given him two grandsons to carry on the family name, a concern he had often expressed. He was probably the happiest I had seen him in my entire life. Still the disease came back and it came back with a vengeance. Diagnosed in the beginning of 1983, he slipped fast. Losing weight rapidly, he soon appeared emaciated. He refused conventional treatment saying he wanted to maintain a quality to his life. Soon he was walking with a cane playfully poking his grandchildren with it as he somehow preserved his rapier wit and Irish humor. It was difficult to watch him deteriorate over time from the robust, hearty soul he had become to the broken, gaunt figure that was losing his battle for life. In the early summer, my mother invited all her children and their extended families to the new house in Brooklyn for what appeared to be a final party for my father. Parties had played such a significant role in their early lives together that it was fitting that he be the guest of honor at one last party. What started out as a good idea ended in a crying fest. My father was the first to cry as he thanked everyone for coming but he felt he needed to go to his bedroom for a nap. Unable to walk up the back stairs, I carried him to his room. I placed him in his bed, gave him a hug and told him to rest. When I went back outside, all three of my sisters were crying and Katie quickly joined them. Soon everyone had tears in their eyes. We all left that afternoon knowing that this would probably be the last time we would all be together. In August my father lost his battle and succumbed to cancer. He was 72 years old.

# *Chapter Thirty-Nine*

## THE SHATTERED LEGACY

THE EIGHTIES WERE a great time to be in the car business. It seemed that we could do no wrong and that it would last forever. Profits were extraordinary, brought about by a booming consumer demand. Chevrolet couldn't make their cars and trucks fast enough. With the increase in business and the resultant success, Katie and I enjoyed an exciting social life. We attended many community functions and became regulars at Fitzgerald's Pub, a new club owned by one of our good friends. We were successful, happy, and well respected. It was an exciting and prosperous time.

As a business, we were involved in everything. Every charitable cause seemed to start their fundraising at Cassidy Motors. We lent our name and our manpower to many worthy causes, reaping the benefit of becoming a well-known, community-oriented business. Personally, I became active in many organizations, most notably the Chamber of Commerce where I served as the first president of the newly formed Northeastern Connecticut Chamber. Through my involvement with these organizations I met many influential and wonderful people and we formed a circle of dedicated friends that shared many great times together. Through it all the dealership flourished although Katie kept telling me that I was spreading myself too thin and seemed to be exhausted. I told her that we were only going to be here for a short time and we had to "make hay while the sun shines."

After my father's death, my mother made daily visits to the dealership to visit with the girls in the office. There were now three girls to handle the added workload with Josette still in charge. Because my father had never completed his promise to turn over the entire dealership to me, his majority shares had gone to my mother. I never imagined that would be a problem because I knew she was proud of the direction the dealership was going and proud of her new respect in the community. In effect, she was the titular head of the corporation, but in Chevrolet's view, she had nothing to do with the operation of the dealership. Mine was the only name on the ownership papers and I was considered the dealer/operator. I asked her once about the shares that Dad had promised to me and she gave me a strange answer.

"Don't you worry about that," she said. "Clinton has promised to take care of that for me." Clinton was Jaime's husband and he and I got along like oil and water. They lived out of state but visited often and stayed at my mother's house. He was an accountant by trade, but no one seemed to know much about where or what he did. I sensed trouble was brewing but business was so good my thoughts were consumed with work. I also began coaching my sons in baseball when they were old enough to play Little League and that occupied even more of my time. I trusted my mother to make the right decisions but wondered if she was being schooled in some scheme in which she was unwittingly being included. I guessed time would tell.

# Chapter Forty

## THE ROAD IS LONG

IN THE EARLY eighties, June and Rick's family, which had expanded to four boys, and our family decided to vacation together on the island of Nantucket. It was quite a task logistically to plan a vacation in those days to Nantucket because if you were planning on bringing your car on the three-hour ferry ride from Woods Hole on Cape Cod, you had to reserve space in January. You then had to reserve a rental on the island big enough to accommodate two families. June gave me the job of securing a place on the ferry and finding a house to rent. After many phone calls, I was able to make the arrangements and in August, we were on our way. Pat was also invited, but said she couldn't get away for the whole week but would try to make it for a day or two. Knowing Pat's love for the beach, I knew she would be there. Her two sons did make the trip and brought the total of boys to eight plus four adults. We all thought the same thing – the more the merrier. The trip over was exciting and we lucked out on the house, which was rented sight unseen. It was a beautiful four bedroom Cape style home with three and a half bathrooms, right on the beach. The days were filled with the sounds of eight boys in ages ranging from sixteen down to our two boys who were four and three. All the kids got along famously and made the week seem to fly by. Fortunately for us adults, the kids tired themselves out swimming all day, thus allowing us some quiet time to have some cocktails and chat about how fortunate we all were to be able to offer this kind of vacation to our families. It was on this first vacation to Nantucket that Katie and June truly bonded and became great friends. They laughed together, shopped together, watched the kids together, and in the evening, drank wine together. Rick and I had always been close and our evenings were spent consuming large amounts of bourbon and solving the problems of the world. Everyone on the trip thoroughly enjoyed the beauty of the landscape and the beaches of Nantucket. Pat managed to come out on the weekend and seamlessly fit into the group. We had so much fun that first year that we vowed to do it again the next year.

Our last night came too quickly and while the girls packed for the trip home, Rick and I shared more than our nightly bourbon. I confided in Rick about the corporate shares that my mother controlled and he admitted that he already knew about them. He said Clinton had contacted him and told him that he was advising my mother to issue preferred stock to her children and her grandchildren that would guarantee their participation in all the profits of the dealership. He said the only objection would come from me and that they would have enough votes to cancel me out.

"Be careful of him, Sean," he said. "He's got some sort of influence over your mother that benefits Jaime and him, but definitely cuts your share in half. I told him that you were the reason the dealership was worth what it is today and that he ought to stay out of your business. Just watch your flanks. Your mother is a decent and honest person. She would never do anything to hurt you or your family. But she's no spring chicken anymore and the older she gets, the more influence he's going to have. June and I will back you. We've already talked about it. It's ashamed it's come to this, but greed can destroy a whole family. Just watch your flanks. You deserve better."

I thanked him for his support and the information, but after several bourbons, I became belligerent.

"Who the f___ does he think he is? Maybe I'll get one of my wholesale buddies from Providence to pay him a visit. They can be very persuasive."

"Don't do anything crazy. These things tend to work out for the best. And don't forget, you've got Pat on your side also. Just stay cool. He's not worth your anger."

It was obvious that my father had left me in a mess. If he knew what Clinton was scheming, he never would have waited to transfer the stock to my name. This revelation came at an impossible time because business was booming. It wasn't booming because of anything Clinton did yet he was attempting to share in the profits while literally sitting on the seat of his pants in another state. Oh well, this was just another problem to add to ones that caused all my sleepless nights. The biggest difference was that this problem would probably not go away.

# Chapter Forty-One

## THE BAD BOY

IT WAS LATE afternoon when I got the call from Baxter. He seemed all excited and yet, somewhat nervous. Baxter had moved back from Boston a year after I got married. He didn't tell me everything he was up to but he did tell me he was trying to reform. He accused me of being a bad influence on him. He thought that I had become too responsible and was working too hard. He knew it would be more difficult for him to readjust to life in Danville because he had been severely bitten by the temptations of the city. I realized he was trying to go straight but he had a lot of baggage to discard. In spite of his shortcomings, Baxter was still Baxter and it was always good to hear from him.

"Hey, what's happening? Are you still trying to make your first million? I told you a long time ago, it would be much easier on the dark side."

"Yeah, but easier usually ends up with mud on your face and handcuffs on your wrists. Besides, hard work never hurt anyone – it just kills you suddenly." I had missed these little exchanges between us. It was good to have him back home.

"Are you busy right now? I've got an important question to ask you."

"No, I'll just kick the head of GMAC out of my office so you can come right over."

He knew I was kidding but he played along and said he'd give me a couple of minutes to remove my boot from the guy's ass.

Baxter stopped at Josette's desk on his way to my office to do a little flirting. She thought he was cute but definitely not her type. That didn't stop him from trying whenever he visited me. Striking out again, he knocked on my door.

"Boy! She's hot. How do you stand it around her all day? You must really be in love."

"For better or worse," I told him and then asked what was the emergency.

"You know I've been seeing Carol. Well, the other night, one thing led to another, and I asked her to marry me."

Carol was a cute little French girl that Baxter had been fixed up with by his cousin. She had been married at a very young age and had two young boys at home with her. She had been abandoned by her sons' father and was looking for a husband and a father for her kids. Lo and behold, along comes Baxter.

"You say what? When did this happen. Were you stoned?"

"No, I really like her. We have a lot of fun together. You like her don't you?"

"I think she's great, but you do know what you're getting into, right? I mean, Bax, she's got two kids. No offense, but you have a hard time taking care of yourself."

"I'm not the one that has to worry about that. She's the one that's taking the big gamble."

Despite his image to the contrary, I knew Baxter was a great guy who had somehow gotten off the straight and narrow path. I also knew that if he decided to marry this girl and take on the responsibility of raising her two sons, he would go at it wholeheartedly and do a great job. He had a solid work ethic and if he put his focus on doing things the right way, there was no doubt in my mind that he would be a wonderful husband and father. The news was shocking but it was also a relief. Maybe the old Baxter, the one that left with me on our joint adventure to Boston, was finally showing up back in Danville. I hoped so.

"Are you going to straighten out your act?" I asked. "Carol doesn't need another problem in her life. For a young girl, she's had enough drama to last a lifetime."

"I hear you loud and clear, my overworked and pussy-whipped friend. I've just been accepted at Kaman Aircraft as a laborer with good benefits. No more bartending for this boy, although I'll miss all the ladies hanging around the bar. We're talking about getting married by a Justice of the Peace in my parent's house next month. Both Carol and I would like you to be my best man and Katie to be the maid of honor. After all you put me through at your wedding, it's only fair that I get back at you."

Baxter had a unique way of looking at things and his idea of a balanced universe included my being miserable at his wedding as his best man. I pledged to myself that I was going to screw up his retribution by having a great time.

"This is one wedding I wouldn't miss for the world. The bad boy is going straight. I can't wait for the I dos."

Baxter kept his word and married Carol. It was a very small but very emotional wedding. Baxter's mother cried continuously for hours. Carol was very beautiful in her wedding gown glowing in anticipation of a new life with her knight in shining armor who had rescued her from her previously rough situation. Her boys were extremely pleased that their mother had married such a nice guy and such a good athlete. They wanted to play basketball in the driveway immediately after the ceremony. Baxter joined them in his tuxedo. I looked at the new bride and she was consumed with happiness. Then I looked at the groom playing ball with his two new sons and I could see contentment and a resolve in Baxter that I had never seen before. It was then I knew that he was going to be just fine.

# Chapter Forty-Two

## THE DEATH OF A SAINT

MY PROBLEMS WITH Clinton had subsided a bit as June, Pat and Rick convinced my mother that messing with the corporation was unjustified. Clinton's argument was that I would be getting too much of a share in my mother's estate because the dealership had grown to a disproportionate value compared to the rest of her holdings. Even though Dad had made the promise of turning over the dealership shares in their entirety to me, his wishes were left unfulfilled while Clinton attempted to work his influence on my mother. It was difficult for me to fathom how my mother was allowing this manipulator to sew his seeds of deceit. She had always been a strong, independent woman who was more than capable of making her own decisions and forming her own opinions.

Each day she would come into the dealership for her morning visit smiling and in a great mood. She seemed to be very pleased with her role and the respect it accorded her. Life was treating her well. She was the corporate head of a thriving business even though she had nothing to do with its operation, and she was the matriarch of a well-known, respected family. Despite the inner turmoil of conflicting family members, my mother was enjoying her newfound status. It was this status that Clinton was using to promote his esoteric intentions.

Three years had passed since my father's death and the family continued to be held together by the strong presence of my big sister, June. She had an unbelievable way about her that people just gravitated to. She never missed a birthday, or failed to attend in person any of her four sons' games. She attracted many friends from all walks of life and provided for her boys a safe haven where they were encouraged to bring any of their friends to her house. She particularly went out of her way to make a big deal of any kid who wasn't the most attractive or the most popular. I often called her the champion of the underdog for her unmitigated compassion and acceptance of some pretty messed up kids. Because of her loving persona, her home was always full of kids from all kinds of backgrounds. Some were quite eclectic, some were crude and ill mannered and some were social outcasts; but if they were friends of one of her boys, they were always welcomed at her and Rick's house.

Katie and I constantly marveled at the loyalty and affection that June would bestow on her flock of malcontents. She was quite a lady and Katie just loved being around her. That's what made our annual Nantucket vacations such a treat for all involved. It was a week in August that everyone really looked forward to. The vacation planned for the summer of 1985 was particularly exciting because Pat and her boys were going to join us for the whole week. With great expectations we again headed for the beaches and restaurants of Nantucket. We were lucky enough to get the same rental house because it was in a perfect location and provided enough bedrooms and bathrooms to accommodate our growing numbers. The weather cooperated and each day seemed better than the previous one. Our last day on the beach, Katie and June were seated together on a blanket watching the kids frolic in the water when Katie noticed something on June's leg that appeared to be a huge fly. June had a birthmark on her left leg that looked like a triangle. Katie's nursing instincts went to work and she asked June what was going on with her birthmark. June said that she must have bumped it against something because it had scabbed over and was oozing a little. Katie asked to take a look, but June was defensive about it saying it was nothing. Katie insisted, however, and examined the mark.

"You ought to get that checked by a doctor." Katie said. "I don't like the looks of that."

June dismissed it as nothing and the two went about their business of watching the kids. Later that night, the subject came up again in front of Rick and me. Both of us thought she ought to have a doctor look at it. June hated going to the doctor. She reluctantly agreed to go when she got back home to satisfy the badgering she was getting from the three of us. The next day we packed all our belongings and our families and headed for the ferry. Once again, we all vowed to return again next year.

After a few days when we were settled back in our respective homes, Katie called June to see if she had made an appointment at the doctor. She was worried that the oozing was a sign of a more serious problem. June said she had already gone to the doctor at Rick's insistence and that everything seemed to be fine. She said the doctor had taken a precautionary biopsy to eliminate any concerns of the family. We all were relieved when we got the news.

Several days had passed when we got a call from Rick. June's biopsy had come back and June had melanoma. They were on their way to meet with an oncologist at the hospital to determine the treatment. He said he would call again later. Katie and I were stunned. We thought she was OK. Melanoma was a deadly skin cancer that came in stages. It was important to detect it in an early stage. We both prayed that June's case had a positive diagnosis. Our prayers were unanswered. June had stage three melanoma and the prognosis was six to eight months. Rick was crying when he gave us the news. Soon we were all crying.

The next few months were horrific. We watched helplessly as June fought a losing battle with the deadly disease. Through Thanksgiving, through Christmas, through New Year's Day – all holidays that were always so important to June – our family gathered to honor her and to attempt to make her suffering tolerable. Melanoma was a death sentence without leniency. The suffering was intense and impossible to watch. Our beloved sister, June, who had been the cement that held our fragile family together was slipping slowly away. In the early days of March 1986, the light of our family went out forever. June died mercifully, surrounded by her family and many of the friends and relatives that she had nurtured over the years, at the age of 48. God must have needed another saint to join him in heaven.

# Chapter Forty-Three

## THE LIGHTS COME ON

THE COMMOTION STARTLED me. The sudden realization that I was hooked to an oxygen tube and attached at the wrist with some sort of intravenous fluid shocked me into consciousness. The flurry of activity in the room seemed surreal. To my left on the other bed was someone who obviously was in far more danger than I was. The nursing staff was swarming to his bedside, to this person with whom I shared a room but didn't have a clue as to whom he was or what was wrong with him. The curtain surrounding his bed was drawn by one of the attending nurses whose face gave away the urgency of the situation. Only muffled sounds of a frantic conversation could now be heard emanating from his cubicle. The horrific sound of a vacuuming device seemed to be sucking the life out of this poor man. The vacuuming stopped. Then came the sound of a whine coming from a machine that had given up. A distraught woman was hustled in and escorted past my bed. The next moments would be ingrained in my mind for the rest of my life. There was a blood curdling wail that shook me to the bone and then a shriek of, "Oh no! Oh, no! He can't be. He can't be dead. Bring him back. Bring him back. Please, please, bring him back!"

Chaos was an unwanted intruder that reared its ugly head on a regular basis in the intensive care unit. The frantic activity had left me wide-awake and keenly aware of the commotion enveloping the room. It took quite sometime for the nurses and orderlies to clear the equipment and personnel from my unfortunate roommates area. The woman that I assumed was his wife and was the source of the god awful wailing that had pierced the otherwise quiet late night silence of the unit wing, lingered with the lifeless body, hugging it in a last attempt to revive him. A priest who had been brought in at the final moments of this man's life to intone the prayers of the sick, the last rights of the living, remained to console the grieving new widow. Others appeared – relatives I guessed – to add to the sobbing and the morbidity of the moment. I began to realize in my revitalized state that this was the real thing, and I was not only a witness but also a candidate for my own family sorrow. Strangely, I felt a great deal of empathy for this man whom I had never even spoken to. We had in some bizarre sequence of events become comrades in life's final battle – a battle that he had already lost and one that quite possibly I too would lose.

After several hours of redeemed sleep, I awoke to find myself lying alone in our once chaotic room. The dead man's body had been removed and the nurses and orderlies had retreated to the cafeteria or lounge to await the call for the next emergency. I wondered if that would be me. I reached for my wedding ring to see if it was still on my finger. It was. My mind was playing tricks on me and suddenly my valuable earthly possessions were a concern. It would seem that I had greater concerns to worry about.

Before long, Katie came into the room. She was attempting to be bubbly and ebullient, but the tears in her eyes gave away her true feelings. She knew something about my condition but was avoiding the subject.

"Where's your roommate?" she asked innocently.

"Oh, you missed the whole thing." I answered sarcastically. "It was better than a scene from a television show. There were blood-curdling screams, nurses and doctors running about with abandon, a priest loudly praying, hysterical relatives – all sorts of crazy things going on. It's a shame you missed it."

"Are you OK?"

Realizing that maybe I was a little hard on her, I apologized for my flippant attitude. My sarcasm had been a crutch throughout my life to hide my true feelings. I wouldn't admit it but I was afraid. I had no control over what was going to happen to me. This wasn't a football game with an opponent that intimidated you; this was life and death – there were no moral victories. Katie was my partner in life, the person who cared the most about my well-being. She didn't deserve sarcasm at this point. I explained to her what happened to the poor soul with whom I shared a room. She hugged me and said she knew everything would be all right. Katie believed in the power of prayer and she believed in sunshine. She was attempting to combine these beliefs in a miraculous cure that would see us through this latest crisis. Her curative powers would be put to a test.

My doctor came into the room – a cardiologist to whom I had been referred – and explained to us what to expect in the morning. At dawn I would be transferred by ambulance to the University of Massachusetts Medical Center in Worcester. A team of doctors would be waiting to prepare me for an angiogram, a procedure that would allow the doctors to trace the flow of blood in my arteries and determine if there were any blockages in the arteries leading to the heart. He said he was convinced that the problem was a small one and that I should be fine. He then told me to get some sleep and he'd see me in the morning. Katie tried to conceal her concern but failed. I convinced her to go home and she said she would although I knew she probably wasn't going to get much rest. With the help of some medication, I was able to fall asleep.

"YOU KNOW THIS WHOLE BUSINESS COULD BE YOURS SOMEDAY."

My father's words were flashing across my mind as I lay in my hospital bed under the influence of a sleep-inducing drug. I could picture him in the showroom smiling and joking with some of the young guys on our sales team. His last few years as a dealer had been happy ones for him. The burden of day-to-day decisions and stress related financial worries had been removed from his concern by his reliance on me. His role had been diminished but the deference for his position remained the same. The employees, especially the newer ones, afforded him great respect for being the founder of the business. It was obvious to all who knew him that he cherished this role.

The image disappeared as quickly as it had come when a nurse woke me in the middle of the night to take my blood pressure and chart my vital signs. Once awakened, I had difficulty recovering the protection of a restful sleep. Before I knew it, the sun was peaking through my drawn curtain and activity on the floor had begun. Katie soon arrived, again masking her concern with her best, manufactured smile. An orderly came and escorted me to the waiting ambulance. Everything seemed to be going at a supersonic pace. I was having a difficult time catching my breath. I knew the driver of the ambulance and we engaged in some meaningless conversation on the half hour ride to Worcester. Katie and Baxter, who was along for support, followed in her car.

"We're here," proclaimed the driver in a cavalier manner. "Your sled awaits you."

I was transferred to a gurney that was waiting at the curb for the ambulance to arrive. Everything was moving like clockwork. Two hefty gentlemen wheeled me into the hospital and rushed me down to the basement floor where I was lifted off the gurney and onto a twelve-inch board. Knowing my ass was wider than this board I wondered how comfortable this morning was going to be. Katie came in and gave me what seemed like a good-bye kiss – just in case I guessed. She said that she would be down the hall in the waiting room if I needed her. I felt worse for her than I did for myself because I knew how difficult waiting could be, especially when you have no idea of the outcome. Selfishly, I was glad they were working on me and not her. The orderly prepared me for the angiogram by shaving my private areas. I was never a big fan of nudity so having the "team" watch as this man exposed me to the entire room made this procedure excruciating before it began.

The surgeon in charge, working with my cardiologist, inserted a probing device into the main artery in my groin and proceeded to snake the device up into the area of the heart. A mini-camera was attached to the probe and I was allowed to watch the proceedings on the monitor next to my head. I saw concern in the eyes of the doctors whose faces were otherwise hidden by surgical masks. There seemed to be a problem. They stopped the monitor. The surgeon alarmed me with his exclamation. "Oh, crap!" he said and then huddled with his team for a conference.

I looked around the room and everyone was suddenly occupied with panic.

"What's happening?" I asked.

The only one to answer me was the young man nearest to me who was operating the monitor.

"They found several blockages," he said. "You better ask your doctor for any further explanations."

My doctor was not one to sugarcoat anything. He was very serious when he told me I had five blockages in my coronary arteries. Two of the arteries were ninety percent occluded, one was seventy-five percent, and the other two were smaller arteries that were impossible to open up with this method because of their location and would have to be left alone. He said the more serious blockages had to be removed and coronary stents, a type of metal bridge that when inserted supported the arterial walls and allowed the blood to flow through the damaged area, would have to be put in place. The procedure was a difficult one especially because of the extent of the blockages that had to be removed. He said open-heart surgery would be a consideration if they were unsuccessful in finishing the arterial clearing. An attending nurse then asked if I wanted to be sedated while they completed the course of action. Already tired of balancing on the twelve-inch board, I readily accepted. Within moments, I had left reality and drifted into "Never-Never land." My father's haunting words again returned.

'YOU KNOW THIS WHOLE BUSINESS COULD BE YOURS SOMEDAY."

The trance of the moment fractured into a hundred directions as I caromed through the surreal images of a bizarre dream world. I pictured myself in a plane about to parachute into the unknown. I saw myself dancing under that bridge in Lawrence, Mass. in the rain, this time with Katie. I imagined floating above our house on Broad Street, which had been moved to an island in the clouds. I was looking down on Pat, June and Dad playing croquet on a magnificently groomed lawn. Then it came to me that they were all gone. Pat had died on a cold day in December in 1993, just two days before the New Year. She had bravely fought a horrible battle against our family killer, cancer. Like June, she was only 48 years old when she died. I could feel my heart ache as the pain of that day came rushing back. She was more than my sister; she was part of my soul. I thought I heard Pat's voice say to me, "It's OK, Rich. Everything will be fine."

Then I saw Rick. He had died in 1999 of a rare form of cancer that attacked the lining of his heart. His death occurred unexpectedly while he was being operated on for the disease. It was good to see him and June together again. They were laughing and enjoying cocktails on the veranda of a beautiful house. Around the corner, I thought I heard the voices of my Aunt Peg and my Uncle Jim. They were needling my father about his choice of a suit. They said laughingly that he looked like he had been buried in that one. My father began to sing and his song was no longer sad. The vision made my heart feel better.

I floated away momentarily into another time. I was at bat in a Little League all-star game, facing the toughest pitcher on the other town's team. I swung and hit a long home run. I ran around the bases with a gigantic smile on my face noticing as I ran that my father was quietly celebrating my achievement. He seemed to be very proud of me.

"YOU KNOW THIS WHOLE BUSINESS COULD BE YOURS SOMEDAY."

Then my beautiful dream turned into a nightmare. Improbably my mother had made Clinton the executor of her estate. I saw him standing in front of a probate judge declaring that Cassidy Motors had become a corporation with thirteen preferred stock holders who were now entitled to a guaranteed quarterly dividend, regardless of profit or loss, and were eligible for their share of the value of the corporation if it was ever sold.

"YOU KNOW THIS WHOLE BUSINESS COULD BE YOURS SOMEDAY."

My father's promise to me would never be fulfilled thanks to the meddling of an unscrupulous relative and the constant influence he put on an old woman. In my stupor, the fate of Cassidy Motors had been decided. The tentacles of greed had attached themselves to the carcass of the business and left it for dead.

I awoke suddenly. My doctor said the procedure was a success – for now. I would have to maintain a healthy diet, avoid undue stress, and exercise regularly. I would be dependent on statin drugs for the rest of my life but otherwise, things looked good. He said I could thank my athlete's heart for saving me from a heart attack. In the midst of the angiogram, they noticed that I had actually grown what he called collateral arteries that took over for the blocked ones and continued to feed the heart. He said it was a rare occurrence but one that might have saved my life. Then he said a curious thing.

"It looks like you're going to live to fight another day."

I thought for a moment, and then responded emphatically. "Indeed, I will!"